PLAY TIME

I unhooked the button on my shorts and slid the zipper down. Then, in a gesture that is as old as burlesque, I raised first one leg and then the other, slipping out of the brief pants. In a few moments my suntanned body was completed naked.

He grinned and followed suit. Looking at him, I felt utterly feminine, soft and curvy and receptive. I knew the hunger I had tried to satisfy the night before was only the pale shadow of the ravenous need I had been afraid to fully admit. And if there was a man anywhere who could satisfy that need, it was surely this gorgeous 250-pound hunk. I could hardly wait for play to begin . . .

Also available from Headline

Venus in Paris
A Lady of Quality
The Love Pagoda
The Education of a Maiden
Maid's Night In
Lena's Story
Cremorne Gardens
The Temptations of Cremorne
The Lusts of the Borgias
States of Ecstasy
Wanton Pleasures
The Secret Diary of Mata Hari
Sweet Sins
The Carefree Courtesan
Love Italian Style
Ecstasy Italian Style
Body and Soul
Sweet Sensations
Amorous Liaisons
Hidden Rapture
Learning Curves
My Duty, My Desire
Love in the Saddle
Bare Necessities
The Story of Honey O
Saucy Habits
Bedroom Eyes
Eroticon Dreams
Intimate Positions

Play Time

Anonymous

HEADLINE

Copyright © 1974 Marco Vassi

The right of Marco Vassi to be identified as the Author of
the Work has been asserted by him in accordance with the
Copyright, Designs and Patents Act 1988.

First published in Great Britain in 1992
by HEADLINE BOOK PUBLISHING PLC

10 9 8 7 6 5 4 3 2 1

All rights reserved. No part of this publication may be
reproduced, stored in a retrieval system, or transmitted,
in any form or by any means without the prior written
permission of the publishers, nor be otherwise circulated
in any form of binding or over other than that in which
it is published and without a similar condition being
imposed on the subsequent purchaser.

All characters in this publication are fictitious
and any resemblance to real persons, living or dead,
is purely coincidental.

ISBN 0 7472 3760 3

Phototypeset by Intype, London
Printed and bound in Great Britain by
Collins, Glasgow

HEADLINE BOOK PUBLISHING PLC
Headline House
79 Great Titchfield Street
London W1P 7FN

Play Time

One

By the time I reached the end of my sophomore year in college, I knew that the whole higher education scene was pretty much a crock of shit. Not for those few who had specific goals, like wanting to be engineers or Sanskrit scholars, but for the rest of us who had been told by our parents that a college education was necessary, something like having your teeth fixed when you're a kid. We went through the motions of going to class, and every now and then might meet a teacher who wasn't completely bored with his work, and might even learn something from him. But other than that, all but the most naive kids soon figured out that the entire thing was a game: it kept a lot of people employed and met all the mythic standards of respectable society.

I suppose I would have stuck it through until graduation if I hadn't met Jeff. The only alternative was getting a job, and without a degree there weren't too many interesting possibilities in that area. Also, on the basic level of material comfort, I didn't have anything to complain about. The campus was extremely pretty, almost luxurious. The southern California climate in which it was located was one of the finest in the world. And aside from the periodic stupidity of having to sit through meaningless lectures and performing the rituals of examination time, there was more than ample opportunity for swimming, tennis, exploring the night-life of Los Angeles, and, of course, sex.

It was because I was suffering a dry period in the last category that the event which was to affect the direction of my life took place. My first experience had been at the age of seventeen with a suave business acquaintance of my father's. I often suspected that my father even encouraged it, so that I would be 'broken in right.' My old man had a mania for efficiency that bordered on obsession, and it wouldn't surprise me to learn that it extended as far making sure that his daughter lost her virginity in as commodious a fashion as possible. Manfred had proved himself to be an understanding person as well as a superb technician, so I began my erotic existence with a very high set of standards.

That was to prove to be something of a handicap at school, for the freshmen who were my classmates were, as might be expected, as raw and awkward as they were enthusiastic. I fucked my way through half a dozen of them before I came to the conclusion that getting laid provided a challenge far more complex and difficult than anything being presented to me by my formal studies. Of course, I harbored many of the conventional romantic notions about meeting 'Mister Right' but I was level-headed enough to understand that that might not be for some time, and until then I had to discover an intelligent means to take care of the constantly increasing demands of the mouth between my thighs, an organ that was developing a hunger as vital as that felt by my stomach.

On the night I first saw Jeff I had been without sex for almost three months, and it was making me more than a little jittery. So when I was invited to a fraternity party by a tall, handsome imbecile whose whole repertoire of facial expressions rarely went beyond a vacant leer, I found myself accepting. The sub-adolescent ambience at those bashes was revolting, but that very fact fed my feeling of desperation. Hank, the lunk who presented himself for stud service, was stupid enough for me to manage him with little more than vocal inflection, and his intentions were so palpably obvious that I foresaw no complications. It may sound unladylike to put it this way, but when he asked me to the party all I could think was, 'Wow, do I need a good stiff cock right now.'

My plan, albeit a little coldblooded, was to spend an hour or two at the party, drink enough vodka to make me really woozy, and then have Hank drive me somewhere and fuck me in the back seat of his car. I didn't want to spend a night in the same bed with him. I sensed, rather than articulated to myself, that part of the process involved my assuming a feeling of degradation, of getting into a whorish state of mind. It was to be a night during which I would make no pretence at being a woman, but would just become a cunt. There was some risk in the matter, for if any of the seven or eight people who formed my circle of peers saw me they would ride me about it for a long time. And although I had no concern for any abstract reputation I might have on campus, still I didn't want to be pestered by the kind of attention I would receive when Hank told the boys in the locker room what a fine piece of ass I was.

The night went pretty much as I had planned, and the party was exactly as I had expected: it fell to the level of the infantile within a half hour, and by the end of the hour the place was like a kindergarten with all the children run amok. Bad music, loud raucous laughter, an incredible amount of booze, thick clouds of smoke from grass and tobacco. I dealt with it with an efficiency that would have made my father proud, proceeding with my strategy. And within a short time I was irrevocably drunk, enough so that I could even be amused and slightly turned on by the bird-dogging that went on in relation to me, friends of Hank's asking me to dance and, when he wasn't looking, running their hands over my ass, pressing their erections against my crotch, cupping my tits.

At one point I needed to use the bathroom and, swimming in a sea of wooziness, I barged into one of the johns without bothering to knock. And what I saw brought me up short, even in the context of the vulgarity of the total evening. A young man in a wrinkled tuxedo was standing in the middle of the floor and pissing in the sink. The sight was so odd that I forgot my instinctive reaction of distaste and drifted into the room, absentmindedly closing the door behind me. As I lurched forward he turned his head to the side and watched me approach, a slow smile forming on his lips. The sense of unreality engendered by all the alcohol I had consumed was noticeably heightened by this strange vision.

'Why are you doing that?' I asked.

'Water conservation,' he said in an even well-modulated voice.

'Huh?' I replied, my mind too fuzzy to make connections swiftly.

'It's a criminal waste of water to use five gallons to flush down a half pint of waste fluid,' he went on in a dry tone. 'This way, after I'm finished, I turn on the hot water and it only requires about a glassful to rinse the sink.'

'Something in me tells me I'm supposed to find what you're doing disgusting,' I said. 'But somehow it all seems very logical. I wonder why I never thought of it.'

He put his cock back in his pants, zippered his fly, and dutifully washed the bowl with hot water. He regarded me quizzically, by far the most intelligent expression I had observed all evening.

'Well,' he began, his manner suddenly diffident, 'It's rather inconvenient for a woman, isn't it?'

For a moment I didn't catch his meaning, and then I saw it, and burst into laughter.

'Want to try?' he asked.

Already reckless, I answered, 'Why not?'

'Well, prepare yourself, and I'll give you a lift,' he said.

Without thinking, I hoisted my skirt and dropped my panties. He looked at my legs and cunt appreciatively for a moment, and then slipped his hands under my armpits and swung me up onto the sink. I yelped at making contact with the cold porcelain, and then relaxed as I felt the heat from where he had run the hot water.

I waited, but nothing happened. 'I don't think I can,' I said, 'with you standing there.'

'Be my ghost,' he quipped, and walked gingerly out of the room.

As soon as he had closed the door behind him, I began giggling again. It was clearly the most absurd situation I had ever been in, and the laughter shook my entire body.

And it was like that, sitting bare-assed on a sink in a frat house bathroom, drunk and giggling that I met Jeff. The door opened and he stepped inside. It wasn't until I heard his sharp intake of breath that I turned my head, and at that instant the blood froze in my veins.

He was the most strikingly beautiful man I had ever seen. He stood six and a half feet tall, his shoulders were as wide as the door frame, his face seemed carved out of granite, and although he couldn't have been more than twenty-one, he had the air of a successful man of forty. But more than all that were his hands – I will never forget his hands! – more than three times the size of mine and emitting a sense of fierce power that almost frightened me.

We locked gazes and for a few seconds all time ceased. I forgot myself, the surroundings, the whole universe. There was only this terrible and magnificent vibration, this rush of overwhelming male energy. It was as though he had some irresistible magnet inside him, and I felt that my very soul was being drawn out of my body.

Then he shook his head, snorted once, and began to back out of the room. 'That's got to be the weirdest goddamn thing I've ever seen in my life,' he said out loud, and then turned and disappeared.

I wanted to shout for him to wait, but I only fell back against the mirror behind me, feeling weak and empty. My stomach turned sour, and I verged on nausea. I jumped back to the floor, and got my clothes back in place, and then used the sink for its more common purpose, to wash my face and run cold water over my wrists. I took several deep breaths and staggered back out into the roar of the party, still stunned at the apparition which had shaken me so deeply.

And stepped right into the arms of the boy – I can't call him a man – who had taken me, and had, through great effort, reversed the process of evolution and become a gorilla. He was the last thing I wanted at the moment, but the heat was upon him and he was impossible for me, in my shaky condition, to fend off. Besides, fucking him was the commitment I had implied, and I really didn't want to be a bad sport. I've never thought of myself as a particularly moral person, but I like to keep my word and pay my debts. Besides, I had come there to get laid, and I was determined to accomplish my aim.

Hank wheeled me to the room where the bar had been set up and we began another round of drinks. Other couples had already begun to sink into couches and corners and the room was thick with the moans of heavy necking. I was still too stunned to feel very much, and wanted just to be alone to bring the incident of that astonishing meeting back into focus and dwell on it, but that was not to be permitted. So I did what I had come to do: I shut off my mind and flung myself into the theater of the body.

Within moments, Hank had me stretched out on the floor, his mouth pressing mine, his tongue blind and insistent between my lips, his hands flying like crazed moths over the flames of my erogenous zones, not knowing where they wanted to settle. He was crude, staying almost exclusively with the tried-and-true duo of tits and ass, pummelling my breasts with one hand and piercing into my ass crack through the cloth of my dress with the other, all the while he rubbed his very hard and hot cock against my cunt. But for all its lacking in nuance, his approach was effective enough, and within a short time I found myself responding, twisting my hips and grinding my ass on his hand and opening my mouth to moan and letting his tongue slide down as far as my throat. He was exactly what I had imagined he would be:

pure, unrefined lust. And I let myself loll under him as he pushed his weight and desire into my body, getting my nipples hard and my ass itchy and my cunt wet.

He rolled off me part way and his right hand went from my tits to my crotch, his fingers stroking my pussy. That really got to me and I felt my legs opening as he rubbed my clit through the fabric. But when he began to pull my skirt up, I stopped him. I knew that it was one of the general status symbols among the fraternity boys to be able to fuck a date in full view of everyone. It was taken as a sign of irresistible virility for a man to be able to 'get a bitch so hot' that she would let herself be plowed before the eyes of fifty or a hundred people. Such incidents usually ended up in gang bangs in one of the upstairs rooms, and while I must admit that the idea had its appeal, I was not willing for my initiation into that particular form be at the hands of juvenile delinquents. I was later to look back on those boys with fondness, because despite all their baseness they still had a kind of innocence, but that night I hadn't yet had experiences to judge them against.

'Come on,' he cajoled, tugging at my dress.

'No,' I said firmly, and in his eyes I saw the beginnings of anger, and I knew that the word 'cockteaser' would be one of the first from his lips.

'In your car,' I said.

For a second he was disbelieving, and then his face lit up with all the unselfconscious joy of a child's. *I* was asking *him* to take me to his car. He could barely contain himself.

I couldn't resist the impulse to goad him on a bit. 'I want to put that thing in my mouth,' I said running my fingers over his cock, 'and I can't do that here.'

Play Time

On the way to his car, and during the ride to the deserted spot that he took us to, I wondered at the situation. From one point of view, I should have been disgusted with myself. I felt nothing but disdain for the boy I was with. I considered myself his complete superior, not only intellectually but in terms of sexual experience. And yet I would be giving him the use of my body, knowing that he was seeing me as a conquest, as a star on his report card. But it was that very condition which prompted me to choose him, for the only thing about him that appealed to me was his cock. I didn't know the roots of the impulse; all I knew was that I had a hungry hole that needed to be filled periodically, in the same way that it bled periodically. And that filling it would involve a series of trial-and-error situations until I found the man with whom I could feel whole. As I said, I was not without visions of falling in love, but until that happened, or until I met someone with whom I could have a rational affair, I would go about stuffing my pussy in whatever way I could, much as I would eat a hotdog at a roadstand when I really wanted steak, but could not wait until I found a good restaurant. And on top of all this was the tingling awareness that I was indeed about to do something 'dirty,' because Hank was seeing the whole thing with such an obvious lascivious glee that I could not help but be infected by his vibrations.

The scene in the car was as gaudy as I had hoped. We drank brandy from a flask until I was practically paralyzed, which is what I suppose he wanted. And I just went along and drank until I fell back on the leather seatcovers, almost in a swoon. In a flash he was all over me, pawing my breasts, grabbing my ass, flinging his body on top of mine. Before I went completely under, I saw myself as I would appear through the window of the car, a pretty and sophisticated girl, her dress up over her thighs and pulled down over her breasts, lying almost spread-eagled in complete abandon, while a young man vented his lust upon her.

He climbed up on the seat and unzippered his fly.

'This is what you said you wanted,' he panted. 'Now come on, open your mouth. Open those beautiful lips and suck my cock. Come on, put my fat cock in your mouth.'

I rolled my head toward him and felt the swollen head of his cock brush against my lips. I felt a constriction in my chest. It wasn't something I had done that often, and my sophistication began to desert me. He pushed forward and the huge thick rod insinuated itself between my lips. And then before I could take a breath, it was inside my mouth. I gasped, and he took the chance to push further, and his throbbing cock lodged itself right into my throat. I gagged and tried to push him away, but he pinned my hands down.

Now I was under him, and he was fucking me in the mouth. 'Oh, beautiful,' he hissed. 'You look beautiful with my cock splitting your mouth open.' He pulled back and I gasped for air, and to my astonishment, found myself covering his cock again. This time I wrapped my tongue around the shaft and began to lick it. I could feel it swelling and throbbing. I became slightly delirious and went a little wild. I started to moan and he began pumping again, his hips beating rapidly as his cock slid in and out of my mouth. It was now slick and engorged and hot, and I could taste the first drops of pre-seminal fluid.

'Suck it, suck it, suck it,' he chanted, and I

responded by doubling my activity, drawing him in and letting him slide into my throat until I choked, and then expelling him, panting, and beginning again by slowly licking the rod from its base to the tip.

'Come on, Julie,' he said, his voice cracking slightly. 'Oh . . . you cocksucker,' he crooned, and with that let his orgasm burst, his cock spurting wildly in my mouth, the sticky jism splashing on my tongue and into my throat. I retched and almost vomited at the sensation, but I held onto my control until his entire climax had spent itself and his cock hung between my lips. I didn't want to swallow his cum but I couldn't hold it any longer without gagging violently, and so I relaxed and let the load ooze down until I gulped and consumed the entire thing. His cock pulsed once more and he pulled it out slowly.

I sank slowly away from the experience and from consciousness, and wasn't roused until I felt his fingers between my legs. My panties had been removed and he was shoving two fingers violently in and out of my pussy. I could barely feel anything at all, and lay as though I were tied down. He may have thought me unconscious and that seemed to be adding to his frenzy. The thought that I had passed out from too much drink and he was now fucking me seemed to describe the epitome of any erotic fantasies he may have had.

He lifted my legs until they were over his shoulders, and my cunt and ass curved out at him, utterly open and vulnerable. 'Gonna fuck you . . . fuck you . . . shove it up your hole . . . put it in your pussy . . . hot pussy . . . wet pussy . . .' he crooned to himself. And then fell upon me, his cock, hard and re-charged, plunging between my thighs. I groaned, and passed out again.

I don't know how long he fucked me, but I remember coming to a number of times, and each time the scene that greeted me was the same. Hank was crouched over me, his arms holding my legs, his pelvis pumping steadily, his cock churning deep into my cunt, sliding, sliding, sliding. I felt no specific sensation, but a gradual heat began to build, until near the end my box was like an oven, burning with friction. I had lost all distinction between cunt and asshole. There was only a huge hot pit between my thighs, and each stroke of his cock was like another shovel of coal thrown onto the flames.

I did nothing but open and open, and even when my legs would split no wider, my cunt continued to spread. It was ironic that I needed to get so drunk to allow this to happen, and that very drunkenness was taking the edge off the experience. But then I thought that if I were cold sober, I wouldn't be able to stand the heat that was boiling in my loins and belly.

Finally, I heard him begin to build. His breath changed rhythm and pitch. 'Come on,' he urged, 'come on, you cunt. Come!'

His words triggered the connection between my mind and my pussy, for I had disassociated one from the other, my cunt building its enormous charge and my mind either spinning off or lapsing into darkness. Now I brought them together and began to direct myself toward orgasm. As he rode me faster and more vigorously, I let the deep throbbing in my twat settle into a single, discrete rhythm, and I focused my attention on it, nursing it along. I began to cooperate with his movements and started to thrust my pelvis up to meet his swoops into me, at the same

Play Time

time twisting my ass on the seat to feel his cock hit different parts of my cunt, also adding to his sensations.

The timing clicked, and before I could do anything else we were both swept up into a single climax, his entire body jerking spasmodically from his toes to his neck, while his cock pulsed violently deep inside my hole. At almost the same second, heat and rhythm coalesced in me into a single sensation of melting, and I yielded totally to it, crying out as my legs trembled and my ass shook and my cunt pounded and the juices ran out of me and over his cock and onto the leather.

I heard Hank whisper, 'Christ, what a fantastic fuck,' just before I passed out for the final time that night.

He must have taken me back to my room undressed me and put me into bed, for the next thing I remembered was the doorbell ringing insistently. I opened one eye and looked at the clock, It was one in the afternoon, a Sunday. I wasn't expecting anyone and hoped it wouldn't be Hank back for more. My head ached, my tongue was thick, and my cunt felt like it had been filled with tabasco sauce. But the caller wouldn't stop, and I rolled off the bed and onto my feet, my legs almost collapsing under me, the muscles sore from the sustained stretching they had received. I looked around for something to wear, couldn't see my clothes, and finally tore the sheet off the bed and wrapped it around myself. Looking and feeling like the survivor of a car crash, I staggered to the door.

'All right,' I yelled, 'I'm coming.'

I reached the door just as I remembered that those were the last words I had used before falling into unconsciousness, and the incongruous link struck a chord in my sense of humor. Ready to let my visitor have no nicety for waking me up, I started to laugh at the situation and opened the door. And almost fell on my face.

Standing there was Jeff, the incredibly beautiful giant who had come into the bathroom the night before. We stared at each other for a full fifteen seconds, and then he smiled.

'Still laughing?' he asked.

My mouth fell open and forgetting that I was holding the sheet, I let my hands drop. The cloth fell to the floor and suddenly I was standing in front of him without a stitch of clothing.

He took a long look at me and said, in a voice that held an edge of amused irony, 'And *totally* naked this time.' He gazed at my breasts, then looked back into my eyes, and added, 'I liked the bottom half very much last night. The top makes you one of the most beautiful women I have ever seen.'

A breeze blew in from the street behind him and I was suddenly aware that there were people passing by on the sidewalk, and even though his huge body largely hid me from view, I suddenly felt extremely embarrassed.

'I thought that after the party you might be needing a cup of coffee.' He paused. 'May I come in? I'll fix it while you're getting dressed.'

I stepped back, dumbfounded, and he came into the living room closing the door behind him. Seeing the expression on my face, and handing me back the sheet which he had picked off the floor, he said, 'There's nothing mysterious. You turned me on. And I wanted to see you again. That's all.'

'But how did you know who I was?' I began.

But he cut me off. 'Put something on,' he said, 'If you stay naked I'll probably wind up fucking you right here on the rug. And I think it would be more pleasant if we talked first. Don't you?'

'I'll take a shower,' I mumbled, and turned to go to the bathroom, aware that his eyes were drinking in my ass. I couldn't think coherently enough to build a quick context for what was happening, but I decided not to try until I had showered, dressed, had some coffee, and talked to the man who I already instinctively felt was about to change the course of my life.

Two

From the moment I stepped into the living room and found Jeff sitting on the couch, a pot of steaming coffee and two cups on the table in front of him, I knew that I was in a different league from any I had played in before. The sheer size of him continued to astonish me, and it was the most natural thing in the world for me to imagine what it would feel like to have that gorgeous body ramming violently between my legs. I later learned that he weighed two hundred and forty-six pounds, every bit of it hard, rippling muscle. I wondered if his cock was in proportion to the rest of him.

He stood up as I entered, and just seemed to keep rising as he towered over me. I'm five-nine and have considered myself a pretty big girl, but next to him I felt like a child.

'You look refreshed,' he said as he came toward me. Before I could reply his arms were around my back. I grew weak and melted in him embrace. His chest was like cliff rock, his belly a flat sheet of iron, and his thighs like tree trunks against my own. He crushed me to him and I realized that he could easily crack my entire rib cage without even trying. His hands slid down and cupped my buttocks, although he could have held my ass in one of his huge hands. When his lips covered my own, I almost fainted; I was drawn into the magnetism of his animal strength. But his lips were gentle, soft, and his kiss was as soft as a falling autumn leaf touching the earth. When he released me, I was trembling from head to toe.

'Who are you?' I whispered.

'My name is Jeff Arnheiser,' he said, and paused, as though waiting for a reaction.

'If that's supposed to ring a bell, I'm afraid it doesn't.'

'Football?' he coaxed.

'Oh, *you*,' I said, his name suddenly flashing in my memory. He had been one of the school's great all-time players, and his exploits filled the papers weekly during the season. I had read of his receiving a contract to play for Seattle, at a starting salary of forty thousand dollars a year plus an undisclosed bonus.

He smiled. 'But I know who you are without your having to tell me. Name: Julie Ann DeWitt. Major: Psychology. Voted by a secret meeting of professional girl-watchers as the woman who combines the most beautiful ass, the most luscious tits, and the most dangerous mind of any coed on campus.'

I was taken completely aback, and wasn't sure whether he was joking. His grip tightened around my waist and I was pulled tightly into him, feeling his cock hard against my belly. I was in peril of being swept off my feet and while part of me was thrilled, another part told me that it was unsafe to let a man, even one as glorious as this one, take too commanding a position.

But he was relentless. 'I didn't recognize you last night,' he said. 'That scene was just so strange, and it wasn't until a half hour later that I realized who it was that was sitting there. But by then Hank had whisked you off, probably, if I'm not mistaken, to fuck you in the back seat of his car.'

'That was my idea,' I told him, looking into his eyes and continuing to melt from the heat of his body. 'Is he part of your team of women watchers?'

'Hank's all right,' Jeff said, 'just a little dumb, that's all. Tell me,' he intoned in a low lascivious voice, 'was it good?'

'Why don't you ask him,' I shot back, a little angry.

'I already did,' he said. Then, without warning, he slipped one hand between us and cupped his fingers over my cunt. I had put on a pair of shorts and a blouse after the shower, and now his hand had slipped between my thighs and was massaging my pussy and ass crack. I squirmed in pleasure and discomfort. 'And I figured that if a girl like you is fucking a boy like him, you must be more than a little horny.'

'I don't know whether I like your attitude,' I said.

I don't know how our little bit of badinage would have continued if the doorbell hadn't rung. 'Damn,' I said, and went to answer it, and was stunned to see Hank standing there. He leered at me, and then his face fell when he saw Jeff in the living room. I saw fear and resolve in Hank's eyes, and he stepped inside.

'Cutting in on my girl is a dirty trick,' he said in a voice that shook a little. I had to admire his courage, but had to agree with Jeff that he was a little dumb. Jeff walked up to him very slowly and then planted his weight right in front of Hank's body. Hank wasn't small, but Jeff made him look like an adolescent.

'She isn't *your* girl,' Jeff said. 'She's her own woman. And right now she is choosing to be with

Play Time

me, so maybe you'd better go peddle your papers somewhere else.'

Hank started to protest but Jeff grabbed his shirt, gave one yank, and lifted him clear off his feet. Then he pushed him backwards and pinned him against the wall. His eyes were blazing. I got a sense of his enormous strength and felt my knees wobble at the thought that he would probably soon be fucking me. I knew he wanted me, and I knew there was no way in the world I could resist.

'You're a nice kid, Hank,' Jeff said, 'I'd hate to have to break your arms and legs.'

He let Hank down and stared at him until the poor boy turned sheepishly and went back out the door. Jeff turned to me, and his eyes were smoldering. 'Now,' he said, 'get out of those clothes. I've waited long enough.'

All my resentment at being bossed around by men disappeared in the realization that up to that moment I hadn't met a man who was man enough to get away with it. And an ancient female sense of surrender filled me and made me subservient. I didn't know where this was taking me, but I didn't care. I turned around and walked toward the bedroom, feeling Jeff's gaze pentrate the cloth and cover my ass.

He followed me into the bedroom, closed the door behind him, and crossed his arms over his chest. I knew what he was waiting for and I was more than a little ready to oblige. I reached down, grabbed the bottom of my blouse, and lifted it slowly over my head. As I pulled it up, first my belly and then my tits were bared to his gaze. I threw it to one side and stood there, my breasts thrusting out proudly, the nipples already wrinkled.

'The shorts,' he said, 'I want to see your cunt.'

Play Time

I unhooked the button and slid the zipper down. Then in a gesture that is as old as burlesque, I raised first one leg and then the other, slipping each out of the brief pants. In a few moments my suntanned body was completely naked.

He grinned and followed suit, jerking off his shirt and then stepping out of his pants. He wore no underwear and I was quickly able to see what my bed-mate to be looked like. I almost gasped in astonishment. He was perfectly proportioned, his legs solid and tapered, with thickly muscled calves and immense thighs, his chest broad and covered with curly black hair. His arms were as thick as my legs, and my glance went finally to his cock, already stiff, and jutting out what seemed like a foot in length from his pubic hair. Looking at him, I felt utterly feminine, soft and curvy and receptive. My cunt twitched and I knew that the hunger I had tried to satisfy the night before was only the pale shadow of a ravenous need that I had been afraid to fully admit. And if there were a man anywhere who could satisfy that need, surely it was Jeff.

He came toward me and without thinking I fell on my knees, almost worshipfully. He put his hands on my shoulders and directed his cock toward my lips. I felt faint at the thought of that huge engine in my mouth, and I leaned forward to kiss the flaring purplish crown, and then licked the few drops of fluid from the tip.

'A beautiful and intelligent woman on her knees sucking cock is the most thrilling experience in the world,' he said. And with that he pushed his cock toward me, parting my lips, and forcing the whole huge head of it into my mouth.

I was totally overwhelmed. Just the smell of him

was exciting, a rich pungent aroma of male flesh. I took a deep breath and took the cock as far into my mouth as it would go, but I was only a third of the way down the shaft. I was stuffed with cock and it seemed not another bit could enter me. But he had other ideas. He pushed my head downward and changed the angle of penetration until he was hitting at the base of my throat. I began to gag and he pulled back, but soon renewed his efforts.

'Down your throat, Julie,' he hissed, 'I want to shove my cock down your throat.'

I started to struggle, but something in me gave way, and I just relaxed and let him do it. I made my mouth as soft and pliable as my cunt, and let him fuck me the way he wanted. He began to stroke in and out easily, leaving me time to breathe, but his movements soon became more insistent and harder. With each thrust he penetrated more deeply. My legs started to vibrate and my tits were pressed against his thighs. My eyes started to water and my brain was darkened over. He reached down and started pinching my nipples, and when I went to cry out, his cock went deeper into me.

I closed my eyes and gave myself up to being fucked in the mouth by this strange and compelling man with a giant cock. I used my tongue to lick the underbelly of his prick each time it slid out, now glistening with wet. I began to want to drink his sperm. My jaw ached and my lips were stretched almost to being torn, but a raging desire had been sparked in my chest and I wanted his fluid to quench the flames.

I started to moan. 'Come on, Julie,' he said. 'want it, want it bad! Beg for it. Lick for it. Suck for it.'

Play Time

I lost all sense of what I was doing. Suddenly I was a madwoman, sobbing, sucking, licking, groaning, feeling that huge cock pound in my throat. I put my hands on his buttocks and pulled him toward me. His ass cheeks were deep and round and firm from exercise, and as he pumped his cock into my mouth, they flexed and relaxed. I dug my nails into his flesh and he doubled his pace.

Abruptly, I heard him start to pant and let out short, harsh sounds. His movements built to a frenzy and I knew he was at the brink. Finally, he gave one deep thrust and his cock slid completely inside me, and my lips sank into his thick bush of hair. With that came the explosion, the eruption of semen spurting from his balls, down the length of the tube, out of the crown, and into my gullet. His cum spilled straight down inside me, cascading down my chest and into my stomach. He continued to cum, and as he did so he pulled out, the jism still spurting, splashing the back of my throat, the back of my tongue, the inside of my mouth, and finally onto my lips and chin, until his cock stood over my head, splashing out its last drops on my face.

I was almost drowning in sperm, feeling it burning my insides where he had begun his orgasm, clogging my throat, coating my tongue, and beginning to coagulate on my lips. I felt sticky and sexy and dirty and good. I sat back on my haunches and licked my lips, feeling like a grand cocksucker. I swallowed and swallowed and swallowed until there was no spunk left in my mouth, and then I put his cock back in my mouth once more and sucked hard, draining him of his last dangling drop.

He looked down at me and the expression on his face was a mixture of gratitude and wonderment.

'Wow,' he said. 'you're better than anything I had even hoped. You're so fucking hot when you get going.'

'That weapon you have between your legs is a major incentive,' I said.

I thought we might take a rest but I wasn't counting on his stamina. Jeff reached down and without a sign of strain lifted me off the floor. He kept lifting until he was holding me over his head. He shifted my weight until his hands were under the back of my thighs, right where my buttocks start to swell, so that I was sitting on his hands. And then he lowered me until my cunt was right above his mouth.

'What are you doing?' I squealed, sounding like a schoolgirl and loving it.

'Eating you like you've never been eaten before,' he said.

He lowered me a little further until my cunt covered his lips, and then he began licking the length of my crack, from asshole to cunthole. His long broad tongue swept over the whole valley, sending delicious thrills up my spine. He glued his lips against my pussy and began to suck, drinking in my juices which had begun to flow copiously. My mouth was still tingling and now he had begun to get my ass and cunt excited. I felt like a leather wine bottle being hoisted in the air and squeezed of its contents. My legs hanging down, my hands massaging my tits, I luxuriated in the splendor of the position.

He moved up to my clitoris and started to nibble the small exquisite button. I was hotter than I had thought for when he began to stimulate that trigger, I could feel myself beginning the first waves of orgasm. I cried out and started to rock back and forth on his hands, rotating my hips. But just then he began to dance across the room, spinning around like a dervish.

'Jeff!' I yelled, 'be careful.'

But he was beyond hearing. His lips and tongue punishing my clit, his thumbs sliding inside my cunt, he spun faster and faster until the whole room began to rock crazily. My mind went reeling as my cunt climbed toward climax. My head grew lighter and lighter as my pussy grew hotter and wetter. I tried to hold on but he was too insistent, spinning wildly through space as he sucked my clitoris and chewed my pussy lips until I couldn't find anything to grip, and I let myself go completely. With that, my climax swelled inside me, seizing my cunt and belly and brain. I cried out and prepared to ride it on to conclusion.

But at precisely that instant, Jeff stopped whirling and with a single motion hurled me across the room. And my orgasm ripped through me as I was flying through the air, my arms flailing, my legs kicking, my tits flopping, my ass clenching. I screamed at the top of my lungs and came crazily in space.

But his throw had been perfectly planned, and as I spent myself, I landed flat on my back in the center of the bed, spread-eagled, my eyes wild with terror and ecstasy. I crashed with a loud whomp and bounced three or four times before coming to rest.

Jeff did not give me a second to recover before he had rushed across the room, flung himself on top of me, and without allowing me a second to compose myself jammed his enormous cock its full length into the deepest recesses of my cunt. I screamed once more, jack-knifed in the middle, and was skewered totally on his steel-hard prong.

Maintaining his momentum, he grabbed my ankles

Play Time

and lifted my legs high in the air, spreading his arms so that my limbs formed a wide V, apart at the top and narrowing to a single point, which was none other than my very hairy, very wet, and slightly awestruck pussy. At that moment I knew I had crossed a threshold. It was not only the size, although that in itself was enough to send me into transports even if that cock had been attached to a syphilitic donkey. It spread my pussy lips until I thought my cunt would crack at the seams. It reamed me as neatly as a blow torch burning barnacles out of a rusty pipe.

I suddenly realized that what I had thought was sexual experience had up to that point been little more than hors d'oeuvres, and that my real erotic education was just beginning. Lying there with that mountain of a man driving me into the mattress, his horse cock beating into my belly with the force of a triphammer, and my being able to not only contain it but envelop it and enjoy it, gave me some sense of the scope of my capacity.

I wrapped my legs as much as I could around his broad waist and pulled him toward me with my thighs. He was now supporting himself on his palms, stiff-elbowed, while his pelvis swung with delicious fury and abandon. Although it almost felt as though I had no operative muscles in my vagina left to work with, I began to contract my cunt and squeeze his cock. The sensation triggered off a higher level of explosion in him, and his movement became somewhat frenzied, although he still maintained admirable control. I shuddered to think what it might be like if he really let go and allowed himself to go wild! It would be like having a maddened bucking bull driving into my cave.

Play Time

I opened my eyes and saw him staring down at me. He was smiling, a warm, beatific smile. Without knowing why, I began to smile too, and then we were beaming vibrations of love at one another while our bodies continued their magnificent animal dance.

'I really dig you,' he said.

'I kind of like you too,' I replied, lightly.

But his face became serious. 'No.' he said, 'I *mean* that.'

I let something flip slip out. 'Why, Mr. Arnheiser, are you asking me to marry you?'

But he didn't answer. For a reply he buried his face into my bosom and began to savage my chest with his tongue and teeth. I cried out and grabbed his hair with my fingers, pulling his head back and side to side. But he only dug in deeper, now taking one breast into his mouth, sucking the nipple, licking it, and then biting it sharply. A shout escaped my lips but my ass responded, bucking up off the bed and pushing my cunt harder against his slamming rod.

What I had feared was happening. He slipped his arms behind the backs of my knees again and forced my thighs to my chest, exposing my cunt and ass most fully. I was prone and flat and open and helpless under him, and he cut loose. He started to pant, hoarse jagged sounds, his long sandy hair tossed about on his forehead and face. His biceps knotted up into veined mounds of muscle. His feet pressed against the foot of the bed and using full leverage he hurled himself into me, again and again, a wild eruption of sheer driving lust.

I was beyond all differentiated feeling; everything was one vast and thunderous rush, a roaring breaking wave that caught me up and tossed me endlessly into the foaming surf of my own seething passion, all the more ferocious for being refused any gross expression of the body.

Only my mouth was left to tell what I felt, and the words spilled out heedlessly, astonishing me.

'CRAM ME!' I shouted. 'Shove it . . . shove it . . . shove it . . . ooohhh . . . fuck . . . fuck . . . cock . . . god . . . cock . . . cock . . . aah . . . aah . . . aargh . . . pussy baby . . . pussy baby . . . fuck my pussybaby . . . take it . . . fuck it . . . bust my pussybaby . . .' And on like that, a kind of rancid parody on Molly Bloom's soliloquy.

But the feeling that spawned those words was anything but facile. It shook me in my heart and bowels and brain. It took everything I thought and felt and imagined about myself and subjected it to a blinding light and searing heat. My ego screeched in horror as it felt itself being torn to shreds by the furnace demons of the unleashed id.

I heard him scream, a long ululating yell, like an apeman swinging on a long vine rope across a deep chasm from one tall tree to another. And all I could do was hold on and hope that he made it because whether I liked it or not, he was holding me in his arms. I surrendered entirely and let myself be nothing but the conscious shape of his primeval orgasm. And in that I felt a climax in me that went so far deeper and sang so far wider than anything I had ever known, that even my terror stopped its jabbering and was still to observe this paradigmatic orgasm.

I don't remember what happened next. It was all shimmering lights and surreal sounds and choirs and insights and para-sensational experiences, and when we had stopped thrashing and twitching and rolling and spewing, we were a tangle of arms and legs lying on the floor. We had literally flung ourselves off the bed!

As might be expected, we didn't speak for a long time. We lay and breathed and marvelled. And returned, level by level, to the basic aspect of perception which human beings have largely agreed, for better or worse, to accept as the common reality.

The first words he spoke startled me.

'The coach would have had a fit if he had seen that.'

I shook my head, not sure where the syntax fit in with what had just happened. 'The coach?' I repeated.

He rolled over, disentangling himself, and lay on his back, his head resting against the bed, one arm under my neck, his other hand curling the hairs in his chest. 'We're not supposed to fuck,' he said.

'I didn't know football was a religious activity,' I said.

'It's energy,' he replied. 'The amount of energy that goes into a fuck like that is worth three hundred-yard runs returning a kickoff from the goal line. Or it's the equivalent of an hour of practice. I don't know, he's got the charts that explain it in terms of calories and metabolism. The thing he told us was that if we fucked we would be too debilitated to play as well as we can. But that if we did fuck, we should stay cool and not move too much. He said the best thing was to get a blowjob. He even gave us the address of a whorehouse.'

'But that's bizarre,' I said.

He frowned and looked thoughtful. 'Not really,' he explained, and I could see that he had become quite serious. When I recalled that within a few months he would be earning almost fifty thousand dollars a year just because of his prowess, I could understand why he was disturbed about the issue. 'It's like you wouldn't let a surgeon get drunk very often,' he went on. 'A man has to be careful not to do things that jeopardize his work.'

'You make me sound like an occupational hazard,' I told him.

He suddenly turned and looked deeply into my eyes as though he were searching for something. 'I've had my eye on you for months, and I knew it would be like this when we got together. That's why I didn't come on to you sooner. But after I saw you with Hank, I knew that you were ready to really cut loose. And I have only three more weeks before I have to report to training in Seattle. I had to have you, and I knew that if I did I wouldn't want to let you go.'

I was speechless. The fucking itself had turned me inside out, and now that I was especially open and vulnerable, he was making what almost sounded like a declaration of love. I knew it wasn't love per se, although we had shared some really tender and deep feelings while we were balling, but his voice held such affection, such warmth, such *sincerity*, that I found myself being won over.

'Well,' I said, still attempting to skate away from what I intuited was coming, 'we can have a bang-up three weeks and maybe I can visit you when your team plays near here.'

He raised himself on one elbow. 'Julie,' he said, 'why don't you come with me?'

I shot him a lancing glance. 'Oh, listen, Jeff,' I said, 'I know I mentioned marriage earlier, but that was just in joking.'

'I'm not talking about marriage,' he said. 'But just to have you near me.'

'But what would I do? And what about school?'

'Well, you don't really take school seriously any more, do you?'

I had to consider. 'No,' I said, 'I guess not. It is a bit of a farce for someone who doesn't have a specific goal.'

'Then what's the problem?'

'Well, what would I do in Seattle?'

'I don't know,' he said. 'I could set you up in an apartment and visit you when we got passes from camp.'

'God,' I sighed, 'it sounds like the Army.'

He didn't reply, but instead put one hand on my breasts. It was so huge he was able to cover both tits at the same time. He pressed down, squashing the sensitive globes into my chest. I felt the heat from his palm, and found myself thrusting my tits toward him. He pinched one nipple and I squirmed in response. He leaned over me again, and brought his mouth to mine. His full curved lips pressed into mine. My mouth opened spontaneously, and my tongue went up to find his. For a long stretch of time our tongues slithered over one another, licking, curving, dancing. By the time he broke away, I was breathing heavily.

He reached under my back and gently lifted, turning me over. I lay on my belly next to him, my shapely ass rising slightly from the floor. He ran his fingers up and down the crack, causing me to squirm, and finally slipped two fingers down between my legs and into my already open and sopping cunt. I arched my buttocks even higher and spread my legs. His other hand went down to my crotch, and from the front two more fingers entered my pussy. He grabbed my cunt from two directions, pulling it open and then sliding his fingers even more deeply inside, and then pulling again. He was prying me apart.

'Oh, Jeff,' I moaned.

He increased the force of his pressure and within a minute he was buried inside me, now three fingers from each hand plunged in up to the knuckles. I began to grind into him, pushing my cunt into one hand and then lifting my ass to impale my pussy on the other hand. And all the while his fingers kept moving, thrusting, twirling, pulling.

'Oh, sweet God,' I cried. 'I never . . . never . . .'

He covered my neck with his lips and began biting the tendons lightly, sending shivers down my back. I was being impelled once more into the vortex, rising from the depths of my cunted being into a cyclone that would lift me bodily once more, toss me through the sky, and fling me into yet a different place. Each time Jeff touched me, it changed my reality. And while I was terrified of the violent changes, I could not help myself. Something profound in me was stirring, and would not be denied.

'Oh, Jeff, fuck me, oh, fuck me,' I pleaded. His hands were driving me mad with desire for more. He was taking me up to the point where nothing but total penetration would do, and forcing me to acknowledge that.

'What do you want?' he teased.

'Your cock,' I moaned, 'please give me your cock. I want your big hard cock all the way up my snatch.'

He ranged himself over me, letting his hands slide from my pussy to my thighs. He lifted me a foot, exposing my pussy and bringing it up to his cock. I could feel it throbbing between my thighs and I began to twitch and roll around trying to get the tip of it to the edge of my lips. He went up on his knees, drawing me back, so that I was now kneeling, my ass high in the air, my face on the floor, my tits hanging, nipples grazing the rug. And with deliberate slowness and sureness he brought his rod to my dripping cunt and plunged easily and lustily inside, my pussy parting like butter to a hot knife.

A deep shudder ran through me and I felt skewered, like a sizzling hunk of meat on a steel rod.

'Oh, baby, take me,' I said, 'it's all yours. Do what you want, baby. Fuck me any way you want.'

And he did that. Once again I found myself becoming utterly passive, an open hole for him to use, and while all the conditioning of my liberal education shrieked in protest, that deep need to be had, to be taken to be owned, to be possessed, overtook me.

'Possessed,' I thought. 'It's like being possessed by a demon, or a powerful spirit. It's too great for me to defend against.' It was not Jeff that I was giving into, but the thing I became when I let myself be empty, a space to be filled.

And he filled me and filled me. His raging cock once more took to the heat and propelled Jeff into an insane ride. Only now it was as though he were a cowboy on a bucking horse. I caught some of his movement, and began to twist from side to side. He was so big and so strong that I was afraid to try to match movements with him before we had settled into a mutually understandable rhythm and routine. One misthrust and he could easily tear my vaginal opening. So I rotated my ass just enough to provide a small counterpoint to his major theme, his theme of wild frenzy.

He fucked me for almost half an hour, and I screamed until I was hoarse and it seemed there was nothing in me left for him to fuck, but again and again he renewed his attack, coming from a different angle, using a different intensity, and each time he uncovered yet another layer within me. Finally, when I was certain I would pass out, I could feel him beginning to cum. He bucked and rocked and slammed into my ass, his cock churning up my foaming pussy, until the climax was triggered, and once again he sprayed a shower of shimmering sperm into the aching recesses of my slit.

He collapsed on top of me and we both fell to the floor, breathing heavily, until our pulses returned to normal. He rolled off me again, again lying on his back, his head against the bed, his hand curling the hairs on his chest.

I looked up, saw him there in that same position, and all at once the ludicrousness of the thing hit us, and we both burst into gales of laughter, so happy that we had fucked, so happy that it had been splendid, so happy we liked each other, so happy we could laugh together.

We roared and tittered until we calmed down, and to my surprise Jeff stood up abruptly. He towered over me like a colossus, and I felt spent and drenched in my cuntiness lying at his feet. He looked down and seemed extremely stern.

'Julie, I don't know if this is right or wrong. And I don't even know just what it is I'm offering you. But I've never known anything like that with another woman, and I don't want to give it up. And if we

Play Time

keep seeing each other, it will get harder to leave you.'

My heart sank. I thought he was going to get dressed and leave, and that I wouldn't see him again. I reached up toward him, but he stepped back.

'You have to decide now,' he said. 'I want you to come with me. And I'll think of something you can do so that you don't have to spend all your time in an apartment waiting for me to have a pass out of camp.' His words were coming rapidly and I knew he was thinking hard as he went along. 'Maybe I can find you a job with the team, in the office or maybe even on the field. And then we can see each other often.'

'I don't know, Jeff,' I said, 'It's such a big step. Leaving school, going off with you up north.'

'Well,' he said, 'where's your spirit of adventure?' His face got serious and he added. 'Tell me now. Come with me and we'll stay together. But if you won't, then I'll leave now. Because I'm falling for you and I don't want it to get any deeper if we have to part in three weeks.'

It was reckless, insane, all out of proportion, and the single most daring thing I had ever considered. I imagined how my father would sneer. And how my mother would weep. But in a flash I realized that it *was my* decision to make, and perhaps it was time to take myself firmly in my hands and throw myself into the current of life.

I looked up at the extraordinary man looming over me, and I smiled, and I said, 'All right, Jeff. I'll come with you.'

But before he smiled, and took me in his arms, and kissed me, and told me how glad he was, I could swear I had seen the faintest whisper of disappointment and – could it have been? – fear pass across the back of his eyes.

But the die had been cast. And I turned my face toward a new direction.

Three

The following three weeks were among the most vibrant of my entire life. Jeff spent his mornings in class, his afternoons at the gym and his nights in my bed. But by the end of the second week I forced him not to see me. It was hard for me to do because our fucking had, incredibly, become even more wild than it had been the first day.

One night he fucked me in the ass. It took almost an hour for him to get the full length and width of his immense club into the tiny opening and all the way up the small, hot canal, having to ease into me and then pull out again, doing that over and over until the muscles relaxed and stretched. Three or four times I thought I would faint from breathlessness. But he moved so slowly there was never any pain, only an unbelievable filling up that had me wriggling and squirming and bleating like a new-born calf. By the time we were finished, I was amazed to find myself bent over the edge of the mattress, my feet on the floor, my full round buttocks curved high in the air, as he plowed my ass with long powerful strokes, driving deep into my bowels until he exploded and erupted, cumming with thick splashes of sperm in my belly. For a whole day afterwards I was giddy and lightheaded, and when I sat in class I could feel my whole ass throbbing, the cheeks still flushed. I was certain that anyone looking at me could tell what I had been doing, and a few of my friends commented that I looked almost manically cheerful.

But I began to feel guilty, thinking I was draining Jeff of the strength he should be conserving for his summer practice sessions in Seattle. The day he left, we hadn't seen each other for almost a week, and that night we treated ourselves to a marathon fuck, lasting until dawn, and when I saw him off at the airport I was too sleepy to feel the pangs of parting. It wasn't until I received his first letter three days later that I experienced the vacuum created by his departure, and my cunt throbbed to have him in me again. My own vacation had begun and I spent most of my time selling my books, sorting out my wardrobe, and arranging to get rid of my apartment. I ran into Hank one morning but he took one look at me and darted away as though I were a poisonous snake. I couldn't keep from laughing.

A week to the day after Jeff left, he sent me a letter outlining the arrangements he had made for me. 'I spoke to a few of the older men on the team and they told me that some of the wives take on jobs as cheerleaders,' he wrote. 'I nosed around a bit and found that there is a position open. I know this might sound weird to you at first, but it has a couple of advantages. The first is that you can travel with the team and get paid for it. The second is that we won't have to be separated at all. And' – and here I could hear him chuckle – 'all the exercise you get will keep your thighs firm and your pretty ass hard and you'll be continually excited from having your tits bounce up and down as you cheer me to touchdowns. I know this isn't exactly what you have had in mind, but it will always be something you can tell your children (our children?) about.'

I found the letter disturbing. Not the idea of being a cheerleader; that was enough of a goof to interest me even if it didn't mean that I could be with Jeff. But that he was starting to talk in terms of years and children. And while he was certainly the most exciting man I had ever known, I wasn't at all sure I wanted anything permanent with him, certainly not marriage and children. I felt too young to be making decisions like that.

But I figured I would handle that part of the problem as I went along. All I knew was that my body craved for Jeff's body, and I was already itchy for more of that dazzling fucking we shared. I wrote back that I would be glad to go into cheerleader practice, thinking how thrilling it would be to be dressed in a tight shirt, my tits bulging out, and a short skirt, with the panties outlining my pretty ass flashing every time I jumped into the air, and having the eyes of fifty thousand people on me, and the millions who would be looking in on television.

I settled my affairs, and within two days I was in Seattle, getting off the plane, seeing Jeff in the crowd, his height and bulk making him stand out among the rest of the people.

'He's a giant,' I thought, and my heart beat faster.

I ran across the terminal floor, and then I was in his arms, and everything seemed to fall into place. Jeff was holding me, and pressing me to him, and kissing me, and telling me how much he had missed me. We picked up my luggage and went out to his car. It was a blue Pinto, and still shiny from the showroom.

'Like it?' he said, his voice tinged with boyish

pride. 'It's one of the first benefits I'm experiencing from all the money I'm making.'

I had to restrain myself from telling the truth, that I thought it was a tacky little car, and as I fell silent, Jeff grew extremely chatty, telling me all about practice, about the new friends he had made. 'I'm only off one day a week,' he said, 'but since cheerleaders practice at the same time as players, I'll really be seeing you every day.' He reached over and put one hand on my breasts, kneading the firm flesh through the cloth of my dress. He took one nipple between his fingers and pinched it gently. My cunt twitched and I bit my lips.

'Jeff, look out,' I yelled, as the car swerved dangerously toward the divider in the middle of the highway. He jerked the wheel around and righted our course. 'Be careful,' I said.

He laughed. 'I can't help it,' he said. 'You know I've been dreaming about your tits all week. When I get the football in my hands, I feel your tits instead. I'm beginning to get a reputation as a guy who never fumbles. They don't know what I'm holding on to.'

I smiled, but I thought the conceit a trifle coarse. To my astonishment, Jeff was beginning to get on my nerves.

'The training program is fantastic,' he went on. 'Pro football is something else again. I realize that college football is in many ways a kindergarten. The coach drives us in ways I didn't think possible. I've gained nine pounds and I'm tougher than before. And I'm as horny as a bull in springtime. I've been dying to feel your body under me, your cunt going soft and mushy as you spread your legs and let me plow into you.' He put one hand on my thigh, this time keeping his eyes on the road. 'I've been thinking of your ass rolling around on my cock, and your mouth splitting wide to take me in, and even when I eat all I can taste is your pussy juice.'

His talk was having a double effect: turning my body on but turning my mind off. We went through the city to one of its outskirts and Jeff finally parked the car in the driveway of a one-story ranch house. It sat smugly in the middle of a bland suburban neighborhood. The car rolled to a halt and I looked around at the wide lawn, the trees, and listened to the quiet.

'Jack Karnovsky lives just four houses down with *his* family,' Jeff said with a touch of pride.

'Oh God,' I thought, 'all his unconscious mamma-pappa patterns are coming to the surface.'

There was no way for me to say what went through my mind at moments like this. The very boyishness and ingenuousness which made Jeff so dear also made him a bit of a bore at times. His taste was so *pedestrian*. I didn't come from a wealthy family, but my father had impeccable taste. Even when he bought things from Woolworth's, they were always precisely right. Jeff had a predilection for the banal, including his choice of cars and places to live. Going from a poor student to an affluent football player did something for his pocketbook but hadn't affected his imagination. I wondered where all this left me.

Jeff was oblivious of my mood, and he rushed us out of the car and into the house. I took one brief look around. It was as plastic inside as it was outside, done in a style I can only describe as motel kitsch. As soon as we were in the living room, he came up quickly behind me, threw the luggage down on the floor, and wrapped his arms around my breasts. His body pressed into mine and I could feel his cock,

Play Time

already hardening, pressed into the crack of my ass. As always, the physical sensations were overpoweringly strong, and despite the fact that I was distracted and slightly depressed, I found myself responding, coming up on my toes so he could get the full length of my buttocks along his rod. He slid his hands down and pressed his fingertips into my crotch, pushing my dress into my cunt slit. I squirmed and rubbed myself against him, my cunt riding his hands and my ass riding his cock.

'I don't know what to do first,' I said. I spun around, dropped to my knees, and buried my face in his crotch. It was the only part of him that seemed worth relating to at the moment. The huge penis bulged inside his pants like a billy club. I licked it through the fabric, my tongue tingling on the cloth.

'I love you like that,' he rasped, 'on your knees in front of me, hungry to get me inside your mouth. Take it out. Open the zipper with your teeth and fish out my cock with your tongue.'

I grabbed the top of the zipper with my teeth and tugged it down, letting his hair spring out through the opening, releasing the deep pungent aroma of his maleness. I pressed my mouth into the bush and worked my tongue around, licking and curling, reaching for his cock. It was pressed down against one thigh and I couldn't get at it. I strained and strained, pushing my face more and more fully into his bush.

Finally, I reached up and unfastened his belt and the top button of his pants. I snaked the pants down over his hips and when they had fallen almost to his knees, his cock sprang up, hot and hard, thick, juicy, and throbbing, pointing right out at me. I went to take it, to cover it with my mouth, but his fingers

Play Time

went into my hair and yanked my head back.

'Do you want it?' he hissed.

'Oh, yes,' I moaned.

'Beg for it,' he said.

I looked at his huge rod pulsing in the air and my legs shook with weakness. Whatever else was true at the moment, the thought of having that piece of meat stuffing my throat was making me giddy. My mouth started to tremble and my tongue started to lap the air.

'I want it, Jeff, please, please give it to me,' I pleaded.

He moved back, stepping out of his pants, and pulled off his shirt. When his hands released me I went after him, walking on my knees. But he pushed me back again. He kicked off his shoes and I tried once more to get at his cock. This time he reached down, grabbed the front of my dress, and with a single yank ripped it off the top part of my body. I knelt there, naked to the waist, startled by the suddenness of his movement.

He grabbed my hair again and this time he pushed me forward and down, until I was lying on my belly between his feet. He leaned far over and tore the rest of my dress until it was nothing but a ragged piece of cloth under me. Now my ass was naked to his eyes.

He raised his right foot and pressed it against my face, pushing my cheek to the floor. I began to whimper and he pushed the sole of his foot onto the corner of my mouth.

'Oh, Jeff,' I moaned, and brought my tongue out onto the calloused bottom of his foot. He squashed me into the floor as I licked his toes, and put all five of them into my mouth at once, sucking voraciously.

Play Time

He pulled his foot away and stepped down until he was at my thighs, and then slid one foot between my legs, forcing them to open. His foot went higher until the toes were at the opening of my cunt. I grunted and lifted my ass off the floor, serving him like a slave girl. I had begun to get very hot, and the controlled brutality he was exhibiting was starting to turn me wild. I spread my legs wider apart, and he pushed harder, pulled back, and then began slamming his foot into the soft tender lips of my pussy. It was painful and excruciatingly erotic.

'Like that, don't you?' he said.

'Oh yes,' I groaned. 'Harder, kick me harder.'

Instead he raised his foot and brought it down on my ass. He pushed down, grinding my cunt into the floor, squashing my cheeks with the pressure from his powerful leg. Now I felt like a snake under a man's boot, and I wriggled and crawled and rolled around as he drove me into the ground. The galvanizing sensation of having his foot prod my ass crack was added to the thrill my clitoris experienced at being rammed so forcefully into the carpet, and I started to pump into the floor, my ass rising against his leg, and then being pushed down and rubbed into the ground. Once my humping motion had begun, he took his foot away. I heard a slithering sound and realized he was taking his belt off.

I went wild with anticipation, and when the first hiss sounded in the air I gasped before the leather landed with a thwack across my ass. He didn't hit me hard enough to damage me or to cut the skin, but only to make my ass red and tingly. He whacked my buttocks again and again, always in counterpoint to my fucking rhythm, until I was pumping faster and faster and he was whipping more and more rapidly, and in a moment my cunt contracted and released, and a flood of energy roared through me, the spasms exploding in my loins and rippling up into my belly. I yelled with the shock of orgasm and thrashed about wildly as I came with uncontrollable fury, my face deep in the nap of the rug, my tongue licking the carpet, my cunt spilling its sticky juices in a puddle beneath me.

I slowly subsided and lay there quietly, Jeff standing over me, tall, erect, brilliantly muscled, his lips in a thin smile, the belt dangling from his hand, his cock thrumming like a plucked guitar string.

Then, as I sighed and closed my eyes, his strong hands went under my body and he lifted me from the ground.

'Ooooh, Jeff, that was so good,' I said.

'Just warm-up, Julie,' he replied. 'Now we get down to the real practice session.'

His habit of injecting football terminology into our fucking was sometimes disquieting. But any man who could shove his toes up my snatch, make me lick his feet, and then whip my ass until I came, could, for the moment at least, be forgiven for small linguistic eccentricities. Or at least so it seemed as he carried me into what I thought would be the bedroom. Instead, we went through a narrow door and down a flight of stairs.

'What . . . ?' I asked.

'A little surprise for you in the basement,' he said.

We went into a large, well-lighted room that had been carpeted and was completely bare except for a collection of what looked like pieces of gym equipment. I wondered whether Jeff's penchant for athletic metaphor was going to lead to some form of absurd erotic exercise, but I was still tingling from the treatment I had just received at his hands and was ready for anything he might have in mind.

He stood me up in the middle of the room and lifted my arms over my head. I looked up and saw a rope hanging from the ceiling. He wound it round my wrists and over itself until I was tied securely. Then he walked over to the far side of the room and began pulling on the other end of the rope, causing me to be raised several inches. He pulled until I was balanced only on my toes, my body stretched to its fullest length, thighs taut, tits jutting out, ass raised.

'Ever been fucked standing up?' he said, grabbing my bulging breasts in his huge hands and mauling them roughly.

My eyes widened in surprise. 'No,' I said.

Jeff walked behind me and went to his knees. He began to lick my legs, and moved his tongue slowly up to my buttocks. The skin was so tight that his licking sent unusually strong tremors through me. He worked toward the center, his mouth kissing the inside of my ass crack. He pulled the cheeks apart with his fingers and dove into the middle, his tongue darting directly into my asshole. I shuddered and tried to dance around, but I could not go far because I held such a precarious balance. He licked the length of the crack and again inserted his probe into the tiny puckered opening. It had the additional effect of shooting thrills of electricity into my pussy and I felt myself lubricating even more strongly than I had been. He had me growing frenzied again, the first drops of cunt juice oozing out from my already battered lips.

Jeff rose slowly, licking up my spine, and as he did his cock slid between my legs. I could feel its approach to my center, and wanted to spread my legs to accommodate it better, but was unable to get my feet any more widely separated. His great organ prodded at the space where my thighs joined, massaging my cunt and ass all at once. I tried to tilt my buttocks to give him better access, but again, I couldn't move.

Seeing my exertions, Jeff whispered, 'That's the point honey; in the position you're in you can't do anything but stand there and take it. And I can go as slow or as fast as I want, and drive you crazy.'

'Oh, do it,' I said, 'do it to me any way you want.'

He bent at the knees and his cock came up at me from under. He pushed upwards and it started to sink slowly into my hole. I had never experienced any penetration as I did that one. Wanting to move, needing to respond, I was as though paralyzed. My muscles ached slightly from the strain, but the extreme posture had the effect of toning my entire body, making me more alert and sensitive to what was being done with it.

Jeff's enormous cock slid into me with tantalizing ease, an inch at a time. My frame shook with mounting lust, frustrated by my enforced immobility.

'Oh, Jeff, I want to move,' I pleaded. 'Untie me so I can fuck you back.'

'Not a chance,' he said, his voice showing a touch of cruelty, but the kind of cruelty that is mingled with a desire to provide a greater pleasure than can be found through conventional niceness. He continued to enter me, parting my pained pussy lips wider and wider, reaming out the furrows in my cunt, grinding into my cervix. I was effectively impaled, and could feel his curly bush brushing into the bottom curve of my ass. He was all the way inside me, all iron-hard twelve inches of him, completely buried in my throbbing twat. And still I could do nothing but feel him.

Jeff grabbed my hips for leverage, and began to stroke his cock into me with regular rhythm. He drew all the way out, the flaring crown lodged at the edges of my leafy labia, teasing me, and when I was gasping with anticipation, he slid it into me again, parting the inner lips, forcing the tiny central opening to stretch to its fullest capacity, and then ravaging the inner walls of my womb. At each end of his arc I cried out, a wordless yelp that was connected to my most primitive sexual core. I longed desperately to hurl myself on him when he plunged into my box, and when he slid out I tried to grab at him with my ass, making his cock a prisoner between the round, lush globes.

But my position allowed none of this, and as he said, I had to stand there and take it. Soon his movement grew faster, harder. He came up at me like a volcano erupting, thunderously and with great force. My sounds multiplied in volume, growing shrill and desperate, until I was emitting a single sustained shriek. I thrashed my head from side to side, the only movement I was capable of. My tongue found a life of its own and licked my lips and then lapped the air. It was as though I had to squeeze the entire expressiveness of my body into what I could do with my face.

Jeff was now fucking me in earnest, building towards his orgasm. I had never felt so used before, and while my body thrilled to the sensations, and part of me appreciated his inventiveness, I realized that our first sexual encounter after our separation had been laced with violence, both with the belt and degradation upstairs and now with the assistance of this mechanical device.

'Jeff,' I called out, not knowing what to say.

But he took my cry for an indication that I was cumming. He held my hips more tightly and fucked me furiously, slamming in and out of my pussy, his cock rubbing the skin of my inner thighs raw.

'Yeah, baby,' he yelled, 'I'm cumming, I'm cumming now. Let's make it together.'

I had been used to Jeff's riding off into his own explosion to the point of being utterly insensitive of me, but usually I was able to get off on his energy. But this time I was perhaps too clearheaded. The separation, the plane flight, the disorientation of a new place, the disappointment at seeing the house Jeff had found for us, the uncertainty as to whether I had done the right thing, and our sudden rushing into fucking without even taking time to re-acquaint ourselves, all combined to make me a little cranky. And now, tied to a rope in a basement while Jeff humped me furiously from behind, I was in no mood for dispensing largesse.

'This is creepy,' said my mind even as my cunt was vibrating around his cock and bathing the shaft with love juices.

'Now!' Jeff shouted, and his body burst inside me, a series of sharp spasms, his cock hopping, his sperm spraying the inside of my pussy.

He stayed glued to me until his climax ebbed, and then he reached up and undid my ties.

'That was something, wasn't it?' he said, over my head, and not really listening for my response.

We fucked once more before going to sleep and after a depressing meal of t.v. dinners. The next day he had to be at practice, and except for glimpses of one another on the field, I wouldn't see him for another week. I slept fitfully and rose early to see him off.

'Well,' I thought after he left, leaving me with the name of the man I was supposed to see about my new job, 'here I am, living in a dumb suburb, with a dumb football player.' I bit my lip when I thought of Jeff in those terms, and immediately tears of regret and self-pity came to my eyes. Perhaps I wasn't being fair. After all, he was terribly tied up in making a good start in his career, and he hadn't seen me long enough to make him very horny and thus a little insensitive. And, what the hell, I had enjoyed it well enough.

By the time I reached the office of the vice president who was to show me the ropes and get me started, I had decided to put my ambivalence on the shelf and pay attention to business. But a part of me had seen the nasty truth, and it would not be put easily to rest. I took a tranquilizer and tried to put all thoughts out of my mind as I entered the office of Roger Edwards, executive director of public relations for the team.

'He's a pretty cold fish,' Jeff had told me, 'but you won't have to spend too much time with him.'

I gave my name to the receptionist and sat to wait, impressed by the richness of the decor. I leafed through a magazine and was lost in an article when I heard my name called. It was Mr. Edwards' secretary, a tall, elegant blonde in a simple black shift. I was slightly awed by her elegance, and when she said, 'Mr. Edwards will see you now,' I was struck by her British accent.

As I followed her subtle swaying walk, I began to feel a little nervous and foolish. I saw myself as a college dropout with hot pants for a football hero following him to his training camp and becoming cheerleader just so I could get a taste of his cock once a week. It all seemed, from a certain point of view, horribly gauche, and once again the suspicion that Jeff, for all his prowess and surface intelligence was basically a clod started to gnaw at my mind. Shamefully, I felt embarrassed about being identified with him.

'Ah, Miss DeWitt,' said a deep and cultured voice as I stepped into what at first glance seemed to be a suite of rooms. I looked in the direction of the voice, and took a small step back as a tall, slim, dark man of about forty-five, with perfectly barbered silver hair, and wearing an immaculately tailored suit came toward me. He wore a thin moustache and goatee, giving him a distinctly diabolical look.

'I'm so happy to meet you,' he said, dismissing his secretary with a wave of his hand. He looked into my eyes, at my tits, at my crotch, down my legs, and then back into my eyes, letting me know that he had completely undressed me, and also telling me that he wanted me to know he had done it. The entire transaction took no more than two seconds, but it gave me a sense of how sharp he was. It was an extremely suave come-on, and I couldn't help but feel a little flattered, although I knew he had no interest in anything but my body. His approach also gave me a feeling I had been missing: it made me think of myself as a woman of the world and not a scatter-brained schoolgirl.

'I'm sure you could do with a drink,' he said. 'Why don't you have a seat while I make us a couple of martinis.'

I had never had a martini in my life, but I wasn't

Play Time

about to mention that. 'A martini will be fine,' I said, feeling like an idiot.

He motioned me to a long low couch, and I sat on the edge of the cushions, my nervousness mixed with an anticipation that had to do with more than the job. He turned his back to me and took a good deal of time making the drinks. Finally, he spun around and started toward me, a glass in each hand. And when he looked at me his gaze went directly up my dress which was now above my knees. I pulled it down out of reflex habit. He saw that, saw me looking at him, and then he smiled. He was playing me like a fish, and I knew it, and was a bit miffed, but for some reason the anger seemed to be directed at myself.

He sat down next to me, handed me a glass, held his own up in indication of a toast, and said, 'Well, here's to a new relationship. May it be profitable, educational, and entertaining.'

I wanted desperately to say something clever, but all I could do was lift my glass in reply, and sip at my drink. Unhappily, I was distracted by the unaccustomed taste and the liquid went down the wrong opening in my throat. I sputtered and started coughing, and on top of that began to blush furiously.

Mr. Edwards lifted the glass gingerly out of my hand, put it on the table in front of us, and gently patted my back.

'My dear girl,' he said, 'do be careful.'

I coughed for what seemed an eternity until the spasm subsided, but when I finished, his hand did not leave my back, but began stroking my spine between the shoulder blades, softly, easily, as though we were old friends and he was just exercising a gesture of warmth. I was less surprised by the rapidity with which he moved in on me than the acquiescence I exhibited. I suppose it was a relief to be with a man in total control of himself after experiencing Jeff's blitzkrieg tactics, but more than that, my decision to quit school and swing out on this larking adventure had started a process in me which did not end with Jeff. He started a process which he might not be great enough to encompass.

Finally, when I was calm again, he took his hand away, trailing his fingers over the back of my dress and momentarily caressing my neck, sending sharp thrills down to my crotch. He regarded me for a long moment and then said, 'I understand that you're Jeff Arnheiser's *girl*.' He put an intonation on the last word which made me feel as though I had been described as someone's pet poodle. I wanted to protest but there was nothing in his words to protest against. I was indeed Jeff's girl.

'Jeff is a very nice *boy*,' he continued, again pitching his voice so that 'boy' was emphasized and contrasted against its implied opposite: there was no doubt that Mr. Edwards was letting me know that he didn't consider Jeff a man. 'He has a great career ahead of him, and *we* are hoping he will become one of our star ends.'

That was the third time he had underlined a word and this time I had to react. 'Who is *we*?' I asked, trying to sound nettled.

'Why . . . *us*,' he said, waving his hand to indicate the luxurious offices, the building, and the entire multi-million dollar empire. 'The owners, of course.' I got a whiff of the wealth he represented and suddenly Jeff's forty-thousand-dollar-a-year salary shrank into insignificance. He leaned toward me confidentially and added, 'You've made a major decision

Play Time

in following him here. A girl with your background would probably have done better to finish college. Perhaps when this fling is over you will see the wisdom of doing just that.'

My face grew red, not only because he had put his finger on my secret doubt, but because he spoke in the same cool, impersonal tones my father would have used. 'I don't see what my private life has to do with coming here for a job,' I shot out at him.

'Well, we've made a fairly substantial investment in Jeff,' he told me, 'and of course we made it a point to investigate the woman he suddenly took it upon himself to bring with him. He's a very impetuous youth, but we would prefer that he channeled his energy into playing ball instead of attaining cosmic orgasms.'

'How do you know what kind of orgasms Jeff and I have?' I said, my voice almost cracking.

'He's been quite voluble in the locker room,' Mr. Edwards said quietly. 'There is probably not a person on the team who doesn't know your cunt through vicarious pleasure.'

I could feel my pulse pounding, and I was torn between an intense desire to run out of the room and to stay and hear exactly what else this man knew about me. And not only this man, but at least sixty-five others. Just how explicit had Jeff been?

'Above all else,' he went on as he leaned back against the couch, 'we are all committed to the concept of the *team*. We have specialized jobs and we have our star performers, but if we are to remain successful, we must all pull . . . or if you prefer, push . . . together. We can't afford to have any element among us which is too head-strong and individualistic. I am saying this not to demean you, but to disabuse you right away of any notions you may have concerning standards of privacy which do not apply in this context.'

He reached over and patted my knee, and his hand rested there as he continued, 'But I don't want to overwhelm you with too much too quickly. After you've been with us a while, you'll understand these things for yourself.'

'Just what are you implying, Mr. Edwards?' I asked, aware that his hand was quite cool on my thigh.

'Call me Roger, please,' he said. And then went on, 'I'm not really implying anything you probably haven't thought about yourself. But for now, I really think we don't need to do anything but have you try on your uniform and tell you where and when to report for practice.'

He went to the other side of the room, reached into a desk drawer, and took out a small package. 'There's a bathroom over there,' he said. 'Put this on and let's see how you look in it.'

'Here?' I asked, 'Is that necessary?'

'Judging from what I have seen of your body, I'm sure you'll do just fine. But one of my prerogatives is to check out how our cheerleaders will look in uniform. You'll forgive me if I pull rank a bit and insist on it.'

There seemed to be little else I could do, so I took the package and went into the bathroom to change. It was a stunning room, over fifteen feet long and almost as wide, with a sunken tile and black tile halfway up to the ceiling, with red velvet wallpaper above that. I took off my clothes and took stock of my situation. It was obvious that Mr. Edwards . . . Roger . . . was leading me rapidly and easily to bed.

Play Time

Something in me felt I should resist, but I couldn't find a peg to hang any resistance on. He was intelligent, good-looking in a diabolic way, very affluent, and extraordinarily smooth, even more so that Manfred, the man who had relieved me of my virginity in so sophisticated a fashion.

I pulled on the bright red shirt with the team's name on it, wondering if I should be wearing a bra. My tits were seized by the clingy material and bulged boldly out, the nipples sharply outlined, even down to the small ridges in the aureole. Underneath went a pair of brief panties, and over that a small flare skirt that barely covered the bottom of my ass and cunt. I decided to leave my shoes off and walked out like that into the office, breasts swaying and feet bare.

He watched me closely as I walked across the space to him. He was smoking a long cigarette rolled in black paper, and holding his martini glass. His eyes registered one long process of evaluation. He exuded a dry eroticism which made me feel as though I was dripping wet. I had never felt so naked in front of a man.

'You give promise of being very interesting,' he said in an even voice.

'Christ,' I thought, 'can't he even give me a compliment without having it sound like a stock-market report?'

'Turn around,' he said.

I faced away from him and let him see my back. I could literally feel his gaze inspecting my thighs, invading my ass crack, taking in the curve of my spine, drinking in my hair.

'Now face me,' he said, 'and raise your arms high over your head.'

Play Time

When I did it, of course, my tits were raised and thrust forward, making it appear that they were reaching out for him. His eyes glinted, and I saw his glance graze my nipples, jump to my flat belly, and rest on my crotch. The position had the effect of raising the skirt, and I knew that there was nothing between my cunt and him but a wispy bit of white silk. I knew that my bush was creating a black bulge between my thighs, and I felt my pussy quicken.

'Can I put them down now?' I asked sarcastically, my only successful attempt at equality with him.

'Of course,' he said, and smiled, a humorless expression which did nothing more than to exhibit his long white teeth.

'Why not change back into your regular clothes,' he said.

I went back into the bathroom and reversed the process, climbing back into my shoes and dress. I felt ravished, and tingled with an odd excitement. It was erotic, but not in any animal way. He had appealed to some deeper quality of female sexuality in me, a more cerebral quality. I realized that being fucked by Roger would be like taking a trigonometry lesson.

I went out and found him sitting behind his desk. The light poured in from the window behind him and he looked like a silhouette of himself. I walked over to him and he handed me a slip of paper. 'This is the place you will go to tomorrow,' he said, 'and meet your fellow cheerleaders. They've all been on the team a while so they can fill you in completely, and tell you things from a woman's viewpoint. After all, a man can only go so far in his perception of reality.'

All at once, I knew I would let him have me.

My reserve, not too strong in the first place, simply dissolved and I saw that I was actually anxious to find out what this man could teach me. His obvious success, his perfect style, made me desirous to put myself in his hands.

He watched me for a long silent interval, then stood up. 'That takes care of our business,' he said. 'But I imagine there are other areas of relationship we might profitably explore.'

'What do you suggest?' I asked.

'Lunch first,' he said, 'and then a visit to my apartment. I have a duplex in the Sutter building.'

I had only been to the city once before, but I knew the place he mentioned was one of Seattle's most chic highrises.

'Jeff will be in camp for the next six days,' he added, 'and in any case, you're not his property, are you?'

He flicked his intercom and said, 'Miss Phillips, I'll be gone for the rest of the day.' He held out his arm and said to me, 'We'll go out the back way.'

As we went down the elevator, he took the opportunity to casually and easily rub my nipples with the back of his hand, and when my mouth had fallen open in response, he put two fingers between my lips.

'We'll find that delightful opening properly later,' he said. I knew then that he was a sexual engineer, not a performer, and would remain absolutely calm while he aroused me to a pitch of screaming helplessness.

As we went toward his car I saw that it was a Maserati. Things were beginning to move very rapidly and were spinning off in unexpected directions.

'Roger, you've got class,' I said as I climbed in the low-slung beauty.

'Class meets ass,' he quipped as he got in and we drove away.

Four

When I arrived at the stadium the next day, I gave my name to the guard at the gate and was directed to the dugout at the side of the field. I walked past the lockers and several small offices, and finally arrived at a door that had 'Cheerleaders' written on it. This was the space reserved for the women who provided the female counterpoint to what the men would be doing on the central stage.

I pushed the door open hesitantly and stepped inside and the sight that met my eyes almost propelled me backwards. Three of the most ravishing women I had ever seen in my life were lolling about on couches and easy chairs in various stages of undress. One, a redhead with enormous tits and long legs was wearing only a pair of panties. Another, a blonde who looked as though she might be a professional swimmer, with a tight, trim body, small hard breasts, and an incongruously wide and soft mouth, was completely naked. The third, with brown hair almost the colour of my own, wore panties and bra; she was almost six feet tall, and as I entered was idly rubbing her hand on her cunt, with the same ease with which she might be scratching her head.

The three of them stopped mid-conversation and all turned to look at me. I felt completely out of place fully dressed, and for an instant I checked an impulse to turn on my heels and walk right out of there. Their eyes were hard and humorous, holding the same look I had once seen in the glance of a successful and witty prostitute who had been a friend of my father's and often came to dinner to amuse us with her tales of the world of high society she serviced.

'Hi, I'm Sandy,' said the blonde, standing up and walking toward me, her tits shifting as she walked. My eyes were riveted on her cunt, and I could see the full lips clearly underneath her patch of fine, yellow hair. I caught myself and abruptly looked up to greet her.

'Come in,' she said, smiling, aware of my discomfiture. 'We're pretty informal around here, as you can see. Take off whatever you like and have a seat.'

I closed the door behind me and entered slowly, my eyes wide despite my desire to appear cool. 'That's Marian,' Sandy said, pointing at the brunette, who took her hand off her pussy and waved at me. 'And that's Irene, our star redhead,' Sandy continued. The woman leaned forward to smile at me, and her breasts moved ponderously to wave in my direction.

Sandy went back to sprawling in a large chair and I stood in the middle of the room, feeling awkward.

'Well, I'm Julie,' I said in a weak voice.

There was a long silence, and then suddenly the room erupted in laughter, the three women falling over themselves in giggles. My spine stiffened and I unconsciously drew myself in for protection. But Sandy finally straightened up, her eyes twinkling, and held out her hands toward me.

'Oh Julie,' she said, 'you look like a pickpocket

Play Time

who's just been discovered with her hand in a policeman's pants. Come on, we're just folks.'

Suddenly, the tension snapped, and I felt myself unwind. It had been a long time since I had been in female company, and I realized that my attitude was the same as if I had walked into a room filled with naked men.

'Do you always greet newcomers this way?' I asked, going to one of the empty chairs and sinking into it.

'It depends. We usually don't adjust ourselves in any special way when there's a knock on the door.'

'What if it had been a man?' I wondered out loud.

'We'll, he'd probably have an enormous hard-on by now,' Irene put in.

Once again they glanced at one another, clearly sharing some joke that I was not yet privy to.

'We're the *cheer*leaders,' Sandy said. 'It's our job to see to it that the team stays in high spirits. And I don't know what makes a man happier than to have a whole slew of pussy lying around in the next room.'

My temples began to throb. First Jeff, then Roger, and now this extraordinary scene. I wondered whether the women were expected to service the whole team, but I couldn't ask without sounding naive, and I decided to say nothing and see what happened.

'How about a drink?' Marian said, her voice low and throbbing. Without waiting for a reply, she went over to the small bar that graced part of one wall, and began mixing ingredients in a large shaker. Her ass wiggled as she worked, two extremely full and deliciously molded mounds framed by tight black lace panties. Sandy saw me looking, and asked, 'Are you into women, Julie?'

I turned toward her, taken aback by her perception and her frank question. It seemed that the people on the team wasted no time on circumlocutions, but much of that had already been indicated by Roger. 'Some of our ways may come as a shock,' he had told me, 'but after a while you begin to feel yourself part of a family. We are all highly dependent on one another, and we spend a lot of time in close physical proximity. Not the least of what happens on the football field is an immense accumulation of sexual energy and tension, and that infects all of us. So we have come to learn how to deal with it efficiently. We are not immoral people; it's just that our environment makes a certain adjustment of conventional morality necessary.'

'I don't know,' I said to Sandy. 'I never have. I mean, I've never really thought about it.'

'Stop seducing this innocent little girl,' Marian said as she came back with a tray of glasses. I took one, sipped at it, and was delighted to taste a chilled daiquiri on my tongue.

'Innocent my ass,' said Irene, now beginning to stroke her pussy lazily. 'Not after the tricks that twelve-inch cock has put her through.'

I could stand it no longer. 'Does everybody know everything about everyone's sex life here?' I burst out.

'Everything,' whispered Irene through her teeth.

'You're going to frighten her,' said Marian, dispensing the last of the drinks and then coming over to sit on the arm-rest of my chair. She put one arm around my shoulder protectively, pulling me slightly toward her, causing my cheek to rest against the side of one bulging breast. She wore a net bra and the texture of her skin was palpable through the delicately scented material.

She turned to me and added, 'You live just down the block from Jack and me, you know.'

'Jack Karnovsky?' I asked. 'Jeff mentioned that.'

'Good,' Marian told me. 'We want to have the two of you over one night after Jeff is out of training and you've settled down a bit.'

'Foursomes at the Karnovsky's,' moaned Sandra in mock anguish, 'what an introduction to Seattle.'

'From what I understand,' Irene purred, sipping her drink, 'Julie's had her introduction last night.'

'Oh, you mean Roger?' Sandy said cuttingly. 'The last time I was with him he tried to talk me into letting his sister fuck me.'

'Did you do it?' Irene asked, her eyes glinting with excitement.

'I'll never tell,' Sandy replied. 'A girl's got to have *some* secrets.'

'Aaiyeee!' I screamed suddenly, letting out a piercing yell.

Marian jumped off the chair and the other two women sat bolt upright.

'What the fuck was that?!' Sandy said as I sat there with my fist clenched on my lap.

I smiled sheepishly. 'I needed to break the pressure in my ears,' I said. 'I thought I heard Sandy say that one of the secrets a person can expect to have around here is not letting anyone know whether she was fucked by her date's sister.'

'Hmmm,' said Irene, lying down again, 'I suppose that's true. And it does sound slightly odd when you put it so clearly.' She reached to the table next to her, shook a cigarette out of a pack, lit it, blew out a cloud of smoke, and said to the two other women, 'Can it be that we've all become decadent without having realized it? I mean, are we the victims of a slow slide into irrevocable degeneracy?'

'Good God!' exclaimed Sandy in pretended horror. 'How horrible!'

And once again the three of them burst out into laughter, only this time I began to see what the joke was, and like all real humor, it was the kind of thing that could not be explained to an outsider. One had to exist within the context to see why some aspect of that context, some specific viewpoint within that context, was funny. I found myself, if not laughing, at least grinning broadly. I was beginning to enjoy the company of these strange, brazen women, and to taste a vibration that I had never known was possible among women.

'Did you bring your uniform?' asked Marian suddenly.

'Huh?' I said, 'oh, my uniform, yes, I have it here,' I replied, fishing into my bag.

'Well, let's dress her up,' she said to the others, and then, turning to me, added, 'Then we'll go into the necessary but dull part of this job, which is practicing the routines we have to do for all the rubbernecks in the stands. We'll have about four hours of practice very weekday until the season opens.'

'It's not that bad,' Sandy chimed in. 'You may be sore for the first few days from the jumping and stretching, but once you get in shape you get to actually enjoy the exercise.'

'Not to mention flashing your ass and tits to all the boys who are trying to keep their minds on a dumb hunk of pigskin, and instead get erections thinking about fucking you that afternoon,' Irene added.

'Do you remember the time Eddie was starting to throw a pass and your halter fell off,' Sandy said to Irene, 'and he got transfixed and six men piled on him at once and broke his arm?'

'Don't remind me,' Irene said. I looked over at her and noticed that the crotch of her panties was sopping wet. During the entire conversation she had been quietly and methodically bringing herself off, and had probably had the world's most unobrustive orgasm. Now her pussy juices were staining the cloth and ripping down her ass crack.

'Come on,' Marian said, 'let's put our battle gear and go out to face our master.'

'Who's that?' I asked.

'Tony,' Marian replied.

'Yeah, Tony,' Sandy repeated, her voice indicated disgust.

'What's wrong with Tony?' I asked.

'He's probably a queer,' Irene shot out.

'I don't know,' Marian added. 'We've all been trying to get into his pants for more than a year, but he just won't budge.'

'Faggot,' Irene said.

'Anyway,' Marian continued, 'he's the one who puts us through our training paces.' She stood up and in an altered tone of voice said, 'But let's get off uninteresting topics and see what you look like in your outfit.'

'You're the second person in two days who's wanted that,' I told her as I got to my feet.

'Oh, I'm sure that Roger ran you through his inspection,' Sandy said.

'Where do I change?' I asked.

They all grinned. 'Right here, honey,' Irene told me.

Play Time

The three of them came toward me, and in a moment I was surrounded by ravishing female bodies. 'We'll even help you,' Sandy told me.

And with that, her hands went to the buttons on the front of my dress and began undoing them, one by one. Marian and Irene stood to either side of me and started to pull the shoulders of the dress down. They took it to my waist and then let it drop, leaving me standing there in nothing but a pair of very brief panties. I felt a new kind of excitement, different from what either Jeff or Roger had aroused in me. My cunt tingled and my ass tightened and my nipples hardened, all usual reactions, but in addition to that I felt an overall throbbing that covered my entire body. My mouth was especially vulnerable to the sensation, and my lips fell open. My mind filled with an army of thoughts, but they were all too slight and quick for me to single out any one for comment. The most overpowering part of the experience was the smell, a mingled aroma of perfume, silky skin, and pussy secretions.

'My, what lovely boobs,' said Sandy as she put her hands on my breasts, cupping the heavy orbs and lifting them slightly. Her thumbs circled my nipples and then rubbed the tips gently. I took in a sharp breath and my stomach clenched.

'And an ass to match,' said Marian as her hands went behind me and roamed over my cheeks. I tightened my buttocks and she ran one finger down the crack, causing me to tremble and relax. Then she trailed the finger down until it was exactly opposite my asshole, and pushed in forcefully. I gasped and she pressed her entire hand between my cheeks, and grabbed my ass roughly.

Irene rolled down the top of the panties and then

Play Time

slipped one hand down the front, covering my hairy mound, lightly covering the pouting lips of my cunt. I tilted my pelvis slightly, thrusting my box towards her, and she smiled and let one finger probe into the centre, entering the already moistened lips.

They all stroked and fingered me gently, not pressing, not insisting, not pushing the moment in any way whatsoever. I relaxed and let myself swim in the sea of flesh that surrounded me, feeling their tits rubbing against my arms and back, their hands tweaking my nipples and stroking my ass and teasing my cunt. At one point they brought their heads together and leaned against me until our hair made a single pool of contrasting colors, and we moaned and sighed and licked and kissed one another's mouths and cheeks.

I was being titillated almost past the point where I could sustain the energy swelling inside me, and in an instant would have brought my own hands up to begin caressing their bodies, for suddenly I was very hot to hold Irene's luscious tits and stroke Marian's lush ass and hold Sandy's hard athletic body against my own.

And it would have happened, except that there came a sudden loud knock on the door, one which almost scared me out of the shoes I still had not removed. I turned in the direction of the sound just in time to see a short, brawny man of about forty, standing no more than five and half feet tall, with shoulders that were as wide as Jeff's and a chest that might have been modelled on a beer keg. His face looked like a rock that had been eroded by wind, pitted and sharp-edged. And his eyes were pure black, and showed no depth or expression at all.

The other women just stepped back and seemed

not especially perturbed to have been caught in this extremely revealing situation.

'That's Jack,' Sandy said. 'He's the head coach.'

Jack stepped into the room as though he were stepping into a bar on a Saturday night with nothing more in his mind than starting a good brawl. He seemed not the least bit interested in the fact that four naked and near-naked women had been fingering and licking one another before his very eyes.

'I see you're breaking the new one in,' he said, his voice like gravel. He turned to me and fastened me with those opaque eyes, and I immediately realized that he had a power that so far surpassed Jeff's that I was frightened just thinking about it. And that it was a power that had been trained and developed and honed to such a fine edge that he could take sixty-five male brutes and run them through bone-crushing exercises until they dropped from fatigue without so much as working up a sweat himself.

'You look like a nice girl,' he said. 'Have fun, but don't get crazy.' And then swinging his gaze to the others he added, 'Tony wants you outside in half-hour.' And with that he spun around and walked out of the room, leaving the impression that a rhinoceros had just thundered past.

'Whew,' Irene said. 'That man!'

'He scared me a little,' I said.

'Well he should,' Marian told me. 'He's like an atomic pile, and when he explodes he shatters everything in the area. I've seen him pick up men twice his size and toss them around as though they were children.'

'If he ever fucks you, be prepared not to use your pussy for a week afterward,' Sandy said. 'He's got a cock like a mule's, and as much finesse as a steam roller. He just throws you down, rams inside, and starts pounding like a jack hammer. And he goes on for hours and hours. I mean, literally hours. Until your legs ache and your ass is burning and your cunt is turning to farina. And all you can do is scream and scream, because he fills you up with liquid fire. And after you've had your fiftieth orgasm of the night and think you're going to pass out, he really cuts loose and becomes a tiger, grabbing and swiping and scratching and thrashing around as though someone had shoved a poker up his ass. And when he comes, it feels like Niagara Falls cascading into your snatch.'

'My, my,' said Irene, 'you sure do tell it pretty.'

'But he's really very sweet,' said Marian. 'He's always solicitous and fatherly afterwards.'

'Why on earth should I want to fuck him then?' I asked.

'Oh, honey,' Sandy told me. 'You saw his eyes, you felt his strength. If that man *wants* you, do you think there's any way in the world you're going to be able to say no?'

'And why should you want to say no,' Irene put in. 'A fuck like that is the experience of a lifetime. And what is there in life beside experience?'

There was nothing in her words I could put my finger on, but what she said sent a chill of terror down my spine. It was so dismal-sounding, so calculating, so *empty*, that for a moment I was gripped in an existential dread. She had unwittingly pulled the covers off my behaviour, off the behaviour of all of us, and the words we had found so amusing before, 'decadent, degenerate,' now returned to my mind with a more sinister intonation.

'What am I letting myself in for?' I wondered. I

was learning a great deal very rapidly, but I couldn't be sure that I was assimilating it or whether it was assimilating me. Perhaps I was in the very process of becoming something, a someone that I might, in other moments, view with disgust and loathing. These thoughts, so sombre and far-reaching, did not, however, go very deeply, for they had to contend with the aroused lust that was pulsating in my body. And it seemed that that, for better or worse, was to be my primary guideline for the immediate future.

'Well girls, thirty minutes,' said Sandy.

'Too bad,' said Irene, 'and we were just starting to get it on, too.' Marian went over to one of the couches and flopped down on it. 'Well, call me when it's time,' she said and closed her eyes. Irene went over to the same couch, looked down at the other woman's inviting body for a moment, and then slowly and deliberately reached behind her and unsnapped her bra, letting the large soft tits fall in on themselves and spread to either side of her chest. She threw the garment onto the floor and then bent over and rolled Marian's panties down her thighs, over her knees, finally yanking them over her feet, leaving the tall woman completely naked. Irene stepped out of her own panties, and I got a glimpse of her red bush of hair before she first knelt and then lay on the couch next to Marian. The two women snuggled up close to each other and began running their tongues over one another's faces and their hands over one another's bodies.

Sandy looked over at me, her smooth white skin and shimmering blonde hair a picture of divine sensuality. Her mouth was open and her tongue running over her lips as she watched the other two. Then quite deliberately she walked over, her eyes never

Play Time

leaving Irene's rolling ass, stood next to the couch a second, and knelt down. She ran her hands over Irene's cheeks, then brought her face forward and buried her mouth in the dark musky ass crack, her tongue darting out immediately and diving for the small brown opening at the center. Irene moaned and thrust her hips back and parted her legs, allowing Sandy to lick beneath her asshole and into her very twat.

I watched the three of them for perhaps a full minute, at first feeling left out and then realizing that if I wanted in to the tangle, I need only go over and find a place to insert myself. I was turned on, but my mind was too jangled to deal with it, especially since it would be my first time with women, and to take on three such vastly experienced females, and all within the space of thirty minutes, seemed too much for me to handle.

I gathered up my uniform and headed toward the bathroom, thinking to just sit there and let my feelings settle. I went into the relatively large room, and was pleasantly surprised to see that it had a wall-to-wall rug on the floor. I closed the door behind me and was at once very glad to be alone. I had been starved for privacy for forty-eight hours without being aware of it.

I tossed the uniform onto the sink and sank slowly to the floor, lying luxuriously in the thick red nap. To my astonishment, I found myself looking at myself in a mirror that had been affixed to the ceiling. I smiled in amazement at just how thorough these people were in their pursuit of sensual pleasure.

What I saw staring down at me was a decidedly beautiful young lady, and I was pleased to note that I didn't measure up badly when compared to the stunning beauties whose groans were beginning to be audible through the door. My breasts lolled easily on my chest, full and round, the nipples two dark violet circles in their center. My waist flared in sharply above my hips, which were full and round. My legs pointed out at a forty-five degree angle from one another, long and shapely, the thighs not quite meeting at the torso, so that my cunt was lodged in a horizontal ledge which ran, when I stood up, parallel to the ground. The pussy lips protruded out from this ridge, and my cunt hair sprouted in wild dark profusion all around.

I ran my hands over my belly, around my hips, onto my thighs, finally joining them together at the edges of my cunt. I was extraordinarily randy from the attentions I had received, and could feel the first edges of frustration which signalled my need for release. I stroked my sore pussy, violently fucked by Jeff two nights earlier, and then put through a strange exercise by Roger the night before.

Roger had me quite hypnotized by early evening. A ride in a twenty-thousand dollar car, lunch in a superb restaurant with a charming and highly cultivated man, two hours on the top floor of one of the city's tallest buildings with a fifty-mile view all around and an almost sinfully rich decor inside, coupled with a constant edge of ironic erotic sensibility, is enough to turn any girl's head. And I had been in the mood to have my head turned.

When I was really primed, Roger had turned to me and said, 'You won't mind if we dispense with the greater amount of the brutish preliminaries a man and woman usually feel the need to go through before they can enjoy what they truly desire from one another? Frankly, as you probably can guess, I

Play Time

have long since passed the stage where the crude activity known as fucking, with its train of concomitant emotions, palpitations, ecstatic rushes, and erratic swings is of any serious interest to me. My central desire at this point is unfolding and observing. My major interest, in short, lies in provoking and watching.' He had regarded me for a long while and then added, 'I should like to use some equipment with you.'

I had had difficulty in suppressing a giggle. 'First Jeff and his gym equipment, and now this,' I thought.

But what Roger had in mind was somewhat more sophisticated, and within a short time I was stretched over a curved board, my head and feet back and my body arching forward reaching an apex at my cunt. He had tied my hands and legs in a spreadeagle position, so that I was totally wide open and thrust out.

For the following three hours it had been a bizarre mixture of nightmare and daydream. On one end of the spectrum was an episode in which he slowly crammed an entire banana in my cunt and then slowly sucked it out, a process that had me hot with the lust born of extreme repugnance. At the other end was his strapping a long, thick, black dildo into my cunt, inserting another in my asshole, and then throwing a switch which set the two of them buzzing wildly. At first I was too shocked to feel anything but vibration, but when the first impact faded, I relaxed into a soothing sea of erotic balm. I could feel myself let go down into my toes and up into my eyeballs. And upon that came a re-localization of sensation, and I could feel the heat building in my pussy and deep inside my ass.

The problem was that I couldn't cum. I was unable to move, and the machines did not vary their tempo, so I was kept continually at the edge of orgasm. After some ten minutes I turned to look at Roger and found him regarding me with an amusement that bordered on contempt.

'Would you like to cum, wouldn't you, you obscene little cunt?'

His words were like a whiplash and I thought he would begin to verbally abuse me, and that would lead to physical abuse, which would lead to anything that would get me to orgasm! I was dying to spend myself. But he said no more and did no more. He smiled grimly and said, 'I think I'll go and bathe now. I'm sure you will be able to take care of yourself. If you need anything, call me. But . . . make sure you are willing to meet my demands if I bring you what you want.'

He turned around and walked out of the room, leaving me literally hanging. I was able to stand no more than fifteen minutes more of treatment and I began to call him. He merely taunted me and said that I didn't sound desperate enough. I cried out until I felt real tears starting to form. I was close to a pain threshold that was beyond the erotic. My whole crotch felt like it was filled with acid.

'Please, Roger,' I yelled.

'Please what?' he asked.

'Please, stop this torture. I need to cum. Please, I'm burning up. If I don't cum soon I'll explode and die.'

'You don't sound really serious to me,' he called back, and ran the water a bit more.

I found myself grunting to keep ahead of my anguish. My cunt shrieked, my asshole was a single mass of raw nerve endings. I needed to have those devilish machines pulled out of me. But before that, to have them thrust in further, deeper, from a different angle, to touch my trigger, to allow me to shoot off. I grew fiendishly desperate, and my voice was hoarse as I called out to him.

'Roger, I'll do anything. ANYTHING.'

Finally, there was a long silence, and he walked out of the bathroom. He was wearing leather chaps open at the crotch, exposing his cock and his ass. He was bare-chested, and he carried a thin leather whip. His eyes were whirlpools of utterly composed and fanatical lust, and I knew then what the meaning of Satan was.

He walked to me, looked at my trembling body with unabashed slavering greed, and, horribly, smiled.

'Yes, my dear,' he said in that same maddeningly calm voice, 'I do believe that now you will do anything, anything I ask, in order to be released. And not only will you do it, but you will find whatever button you have to press inside you to love doing it, to embrace it with total passion and abandon, so that you don't merely experience the act, but that you *become* the act.' He paused, drew back his arm, and struck one long harsh lash across my thighs, the leather biting into the flesh and slapping across my open cunt. I stiffened throughout my entire frame and lept to within a fraction of the energy level necessary for orgasm, and just as quickly, I subsided.

'Yesss,' he hissed. 'I will bring you to the brink again and again, and before I am finished you will be drooling and slobbering and begging me to attain even greater depths of vileness. Won't you?' And as he asked the question, the lash struck once more, this time across my nipples, and I screamed at the top of my lungs as I was catapulted once more to the brink of climax.

'Oh, you foul loathsome bastard,' I said out of a ragged mouth as I turned to face him, 'please, please, whip me until I'm bleeding, unleash all your evil onto my body, please.'

Roger snickered. 'Really,' he said, his voice assuming a sudden fey intonation, 'I'm afraid you've gone somewhat overboard, Julie.' And then he laughed, an ugly introverted snort that exploded in his chest and contorted his lips.

He reached over, undid the dildoes, untied my bonds, and threw me face forward on the floor. His whip began raining down on my ass and legs. I twitched and spewed gibberish under the blows.

'Start crawling,' he ordered, 'crawl into the bathroom, crawl on your belly into the bathroom, and we'll see how you like the actual taste of evil.'

The vividness of what followed had begun to drag me into reliving the rest of the memory when I realized that I was no longer alone in the bathroom of the clubhouse. I opened my eyes and saw Sandy standing over me.

'Well, isn't that pretty?' she said, and I realized I was lying there with one hand on my right breast and the other halfway inside my cunt.

I blinked and grinned a little sheepishly. 'I guess I almost dozed off,' I said.

'Dozed, my ass,' said Marian, poking her head into the door.

'Come on, you cunts,' shouted Irene from the other room. 'Shake your asses and get dressed, so we can go out on the field and shake our asses. Duty calls!'

Play Time

I sat up slowly, reached for my costume, and tried to clear my head in order to go out for my first practice as a cheerleader.

Five

By the time I saw Jeff again, I realized that I had moved to a different level of understanding. I saw that he had served as the catalyst to bump me out of my monotonous grind at school and into the scarifying but terribly thrilling world of professional football. I knew that I still felt some fondness for him, and had no objections at all to fucking him again, but I was resolved to move out of the house he had found for us and set myself up independently.

The week had been exhausting. As Sandy predicted, I was sore from the unaccustomed exercise, but after a few days began to enjoy the exhilarating activity. Tony had turned out to be a rather unassuming and pleasant man, at least on the surface, and it seemed that the only thing that anyone could say against him is that he refused to join in any of the sex games that practically everyone else delighted in most of the time. He put us through our paces every day, showing us the routines, and then making us practice them until they were almost second nature.

The nights were something else. I accepted one more invitation from Roger. This time he wanted to run through his Satanic trip right away but that pissed me off and I refused. He became peeved, and then ushered me out unceremoniously. I stopped into a bar for a drink to calm my nerves, and let myself be picked up by two college students who took me to their apartment and spent the night taking turns and doubling up on me and on one another. They were that new breed of bisexual which makes no distinctions at all in gender, and seems perfectly at home with whatever configurations it can conjure up.

As I lay between them, a cock in my ass and a cock in my cunt, humping furiously to engorge myself in both holes as deeply as possible, slamming back and forth on their stiff rods, feeling the intense heat generated in the thin membrane that separated pussy from anal canal, I knew that, for better or worse, I was following an arc of sexual activity which was shooting rapidly into uncharted spaces. The itch that I had felt in my cunt from time to time I turned sixteen had grown into an almost unbearable ache, a yearning need to be rubbed and touched and stuffed. Manfred had busted my physical cherry, but Jeff had taken away my psychic virginity, the thing in my mind that had me thinking I was not free to swing out as far and wide as I wanted. My body was roaring with need, and my mind had acquiesced, and agreed not to manufacture any guilt about it, at least for a while. It was as though I had tacitly given myself permission to go all the way, and explore the erotic impulse to its core.

Each night after that I went hunting, and since I was young and randy and good-looking and wore clothes that flaunted my tits and outlined my ass, I had no trouble scoring. And by the time Saturday rolled around, I found myself wondering where I would be looking that night before realizing that that was the night I was to see Jeff. I suppose I knew that I would have a bad scene with him, but I was hoping

Play Time

to keep things light, to act sophisticated and sort of dance my way out of the entanglement with him without his becoming too upset. Of course, that was a fool's dream.

When he arrived, I had already cooked a smashing dinner and was wearing my shortest skirt and tightest blouse. I planned to feed him, ply him with drinks, and fuck him silly, and then casually mention that I thought it best if I moved in with Sandy, for companionship.

But as he burst into the house, I knew that I wouldn't have a chance to even attempt my plan. He was seething with anger, a rage that must have been building for days. His face was twisted and his whole body was tense with the threat of imminent violence. I blanched and became fearful for my very life.

He rushed across the kitchen floor and without breaking stride drew up his right hand and swung it through the air, clipping me backhanded across the face. The blow spun me around three times, sent stars shooting across my eyes, caused an explosive ringing in my ears, and finally had me crashing to the floor.

'You bitch,' he yelled, 'you slut, you scummy rotten cunt!'

The words poured down on me like fists. He reached down, grabbed my shirt, yanked me to my feet, and began slapping my face again, back and forth until I was screaming with pain and terror.

'Jeff, STOP,' I yelled, 'you'll kill me, Jeff!'

'I ought to kill you,' he rasped.

'Why are you doing this?' I sobbed, holding on to him, forcing myself close to him so he wouldn't hit me any more.

He grabbed my shoulders, shook me harshly, and

then threw me to one side. I caromed off the refrigerator, staggered back into the center of the room, and finally sank onto one of the chairs.

'Oh, you really can play the innocent,' he said, his voice dripping with scorn. 'You know what the word is around the locker room? They're saying that you let Roger Edwards whip you.'

I saw him standing there, his face beet red, and although I was literally horrified that he might really damage me, I couldn't help but see how ridiculous he was. He resembled nothing so much as a frustrated adolescent.

I laughed hysterically. 'And what about you? Tying me up, slapping me around. And what have you planned tonight – to punch me to death? My God, after your brutality, Roger's attentions seem the soul of tenderness.'

'But you're *my* girl, not anyone else's,' he shouted.

'And as far as locker room talk is concerned,' I went on recklessly, 'who was it that told the boys how I suck cock, and what my pussy tastes like, and how much I like getting it in the ass? Who set me up?'

I could see that my words were getting to him, and he was losing his sense of righteous indignation. But I got carried away by my turning of the tide battle and rushed on. 'And anyway, I'm not your girl or anyone else's girl. I'm not property. Nobody owns me, especially not you. And I'm going to pack my things and get out of this tacky little house and your tacky little car and your tacky little mind, and you can take all your repressed homosexual machismo and shove it up your ass. Or better still, go back to the locker room and have one of the boys do it for you.'

I knew I had made a mistake when I saw what little intelligence had been left in his eyes go dim and be replaced by a look of sheer black brutality. I had wounded him too deeply for him to be able to deal with me rationally, and he was forced to revert to the mode of behaviour which would give him back his ego, something that he valued, obviously, much more than anything that I might offer.

His face became a mask of violence, purpled with cruel lust. He regressed instantaneously back to a Stone Age mentality, which, given the fact that he was, after all, a football player, had never been too far beneath the surface to begin with. He advanced on me like a cave man, his shoulders hunched, his fingers curled, his brow thickened. He snorted through his nose and his mouth was a scar of menacing lupine pincers.

'All right,' he said in a low hoarse voice, 'all right. Go ahead. Do what you want. Fuck who you want. I don't own you. But before you walk out of here, you're going to have my brand on you. And for the rest of your life, you will always have the mark burned in your skin.'

He stood in front of me, shot out one hand, grasped me by the throat, and lifted me to my feet. I gasped for breath. He brought his face to within an inch of mine. 'I don't even want you any more, you little whore. So I'll throw you to the pack. But anyone who has you will always know that I was here first.'

'What are you going to do?' I rasped.

He smiled, a hideous grin. 'First I'm going to use your luscious little body, and then you'll see what I'm going to do.'

It's difficult to describe what followed as fucking. Certainly, all the machinery and motion was present, but there was no meaning. Long before I lost my virginity, I had let myself be lost in the myth of love which has haunted us since the Romantic Period. There would be a man, I thought, and he would somehow be my *other*, my completion. We would complement one another perfectly, and yet he would be a bit stronger, a bit wiser in the ways of the world, while I provided a greater balance of stability, of home-sense, of – dare I use the word? – *spirituality*.

I knew I would be attracted on all levels: our minds would mesh, our bodies would merge, and our hearts would beat as one. And when we wished to feel and express the totality of our union, of our love, we would take to one another's arms, and shed our clothing, and give one another the rare gift of complete nakedness and vulnerability. Then there would be no games, no thoughts, no structure, but the simple unadorned flow of the life energy itself. And with that we would know rapture, and ecstasy, and passion, and finally, death itself.

Somewhere along the line between early teenage and age seventeen, I suppose I was infected with the modern illness which substitutes one model of reality for another without understanding that it is doing so, and thus invests us with a worldview that is not only less efficient but less aesthetically gratifying. In this way I came to view love as 'old fashioned,' even though I had not yet found anything as worthwhile to use as an operative paradigm. Slowly, I succumbed to my father's cynicism, my mother's indifference, and the general shabbiness of life in the twentieth century. And ultimately fell into the trap of divorcing eros from philos, and both from caritas.

The logical conclusion of this line of development now stood before me, a crazed demon that I had to

Play Time

take full responsibility for helping to conjure up. Once again I could only pray that his vehemence did not explode into the berserk, and that I came through with all my bones unbroken.

And yet, so much was I a slave to the pull of sensuality, that even as I stepped back in trepidation, my knees were shaking with muted desire and my cunt quivered in anticipation. I had a picture of myself, lips trembling, backing away, my eyes wide in horror, while my nipples hardened under the cloth of my blouse and my thighs flashed beneath the miniskirt. When I saw the gleam of lust in his eyes, I relaxed a bit, for it meant that libido had begun to take the reins away form mortido.

As he passed the kitchen table, he picked up a long wicked-looking carving knife. I gasped. He lunged forward with his left hand and grabbed me by the belt. I was pulled tightly up against him, and grew weak as I was flooded with his powerful vibrations.

'Don't kill me,' I pleaded.

'No, Julie,' he said, 'I'm not crazy. Just pissed off.'

And with that he brought the knife between us and slid it under my skirt, yanked upward and cut the fabric neatly. It fell to the floor and I was nude from the waist down, my pussy suddenly shy in the light. He reached the knife behind me and slit the shirt down the back, and then pulled it off from in front. Now I had nothing on, and he was fully dressed.

He pushed me hard and I stumbled and fell on the cold kitchen linoleum. He stood over me and slowly unzipped his pants, and let his cock spring out. It was three-quarters hard and stiffening. As always, I was overwhelmed by its sheer mass.

'You're such a little slut,' he said as he saw me

involuntarily squirm on the floor. 'Go ahead, rub your pretty little ass on the ground and get yourself hot. It'll save me the trouble of getting you wet. Come on, stick your finger in your slit and slosh it around. I want to hear your pussy gargle.'

I fixed in my mind the idea that what was happening was not something I should identify with, that I could take the experience so long as I didn't let it wipe out my deeper and as yet untested sense of what sex is about. The reason Roger had so intensely attracted and then repelled me was that he was not satisfied with behavior, he wanted total commitment. The body was not enough for his jaded sensibilities, he needed to rape the soul. And yet, what was he looking for except what we all wanted: the totality of love.

Jeff knelt down between my thighs and watched with smoldering eyes as I slipped two fingers into my cunt and began sliding them in and out. The slim pussy lips parted around my hand, fluttering as I rubbed in and out, and by the third stroke, my fingers were already glistening with secretions. I brought my other hand around and took the lips of my cunt in my fingers and pulled in opposite directions, spreading the hole wide, letting him see the pink inner petals and the serrated tiny hole.

'This is cunt,' I thought, 'this is my cunt. And it has sent his mammoth of a man into paroxysms of jealousy and anger, and had now brought him to his knees.'

My cunt parted like a great blind eye, sensitive but unseeing. I closed my eyes and let my cunt become the central organ of perception. It reached out its sensors, it quivered with radar vibrations, beaming out toward the beacon of his cock, and relaying messages of heat and proximity. My cunt could feel his cock approaching, knew when it moved in close, was aware of the angle.

'Julie,' Jeff said in a strangled voice, 'I . . .'

But the words didn't come, and for an instant I hovered on the brink of submission. I knew that if I wanted, I could *have* this man, could let him into me and let that entrance be the mark of possession. He would posses me, but I would also own him. And if he had been another man, a man I had never seen and didn't know existed, a man who brought to life the as-yet-unformed image of the one who was my true mate, I would have opened my eyes, and offered my lips, and given my heart.

But Jeff was not the one, and I knew that the pain and violence we had shared was simply the anger born of realizing that no matter how deeply we fucked, the primal connection would not be made.

Thus, with cold-blooded awareness, I rejected the implied request in his tone, and instead screwed myself into hardness and whispered, out of the corners of my mouth, 'Come on, you cock stud, shove that hunk of meat inside me and stuff me with sperm.'

There was a moment of skewed silence, and then he exploded, 'You rotten whore, you slimy bitch, you cunt, you scum,' and with that plowed his rod straight into the farthest recesses of my twat.

I gasped for air and my legs jacknifed high above my head. He drove mercilessly into the folds of my pussy, and his entrance was like a stab from a knife.

'Arghh,' I moaned and brought my hands up to his shoulders. But he slapped them away. 'Don't touch me,' he said, 'I don't want to touch any part of you but your hole. That's the only thing you're interested in, isn't it?'

His words cleared the way for him to rape me, and that is the only way to describe what happened. He would not let me enjoy a moment of it. Each time I veered toward pleasure, he turned me to one side, or tilted my legs at a different angle. He shifted his weight so he could bear down on me with full power, and his enormous cock, growing out of his powerful body, beat into me with a terrible rhythm. He slammed into my snatch, pumping furiously, driving my ass into the floor. He took his hands off the tiles and pressed them down on my breasts, letting the full weight of his upper body drive into my tits, squashing the round orbs onto my chest, grinding the nipples.

When he had had enough of that he pulled out and roughly turned me over, exposing my bare ass to his lust. I didn't think he would do what he did then, for he had not lubricated my asshole at all. But he guided the tip of his cock to the small opening, and then pierced.

When my eyes opened, he pushed my shoulders into the floor, rocked back on his thighs, and grabbed my hips with his hands. My ass was curved high, ravished and gasping. I imagined that this is what it would feel like to lose one's virginity to a man who didn't know how to be gentle, and while Manfred had parted my maidenhead with the most delicate ease, I felt I was now paying the karmic dues I had coming to me.

Jeff's huge hands tightened and he clasped me firmly, lifting my ass off the ground. And then he used it to masturbate with. Holding me lightly, he lifted and dropped and rotated and shifted my buttocks so that I did a dance around his cock, but no movement that I was responsible for. In one sense it was highly degrading, to have my bottom used simply as a hand to bring him off. But in addition, and partly because of that, the thing became very erotic.

As my sphincter muscles relaxed, I began to feel the glow of pleasure in the sensations, and could allow myself the laziness of just letting him run the entire number. I could hear him breathing more heavily, panting. He pulled me into him until his balls slapped against my pussy and his bush rubbed into my ass crack, the head of his cock rodding up to my belly, while the thick base of the shaft stretched my asshole to the limit.

'God but it feels good to have a cock up my ass,' I thought to myself, 'no matter what the circumstances.'

But Jeff was determined to take his climax without giving me pleasure. There was really only one thing left for him to do, and he pulled out of me sharply, leaving me gaping like a landed fish, the sudden void between my cheeks throbbing with desire to be filled.

He put one arm under me and threw me over onto my back. I flopped over and in a flash he was on top of me, his knees into my armpits, his cock pulsating over my face.

'Lick it,' he ordered.

'Now,' he said, and tilted forward, bringing the prick to my lips. He pushed forward and it slid slowly into my mouth. He took each of my hands in one of his, and pinned my arms over my head. He leaned into me and started fucking my mouth. I tried to turn my face away but he was too strong, his rod like an iron bar prying my jaws apart, pressing my tongue down, opening my throat.

'Now,' he repeated, 'you little cocksucker, you little tramp, take it in the mouth.'

My lips flapped back and forth as he slid in and out of me, and his cock plunged more deeply into my throat. My legs curled and my knees hit against his back. My cunt opened and my asshole throbbed. He had done what he had wanted, reduced me to the status of open hole, and now he was taking revenge for what he felt was a terrible injury to his ego, but was really more serious than that, a refusal to accept him as my man.

'Fuck you . . . fuck . . . mouth . . . bitch . . .' he chanted as his ass flexed and he drove his hips forward ramming his hot rod down my throat. I began to gag because he didn't leave me time to breathe, and each time my stomach convulsed I could feel the thin vomit rising in my gorge. He was relentless, and kept pressing, until I was retching around his cock. At once he pulled out, leaving me gasping. To my astonishment, my tongue shot out and began to lap the air while my mouth made sucking noises. It was as though he had pressed a reflex button which triggered me into sucking motions. Following the James-Lange notion, the movement gave birth to the feelings, and suddenly I was hungry to have his cock in my mouth again. I reached up but my head could only come a few inches off the floor.

'Aahhh,' I moaned, trying to lick the underbelly of his cock.

'Beg me,' he said.

In reply I ran my tongue over my lips, wetting them lasciviously, and curled my tongue toward him, flicking it back and forth. I offered him a face of cocksucking salaciousness, silently imploring him to

Play Time

fuck my mouth and have it be all the dirty things that were going through his mind.

He released my hands and sat down on my tits, his hard buttocks flattening the soft squishy breasts into my chest. I reached my head forward, but he pushed it back. 'If you move, I'll slug you,' he said.

And then he wrapped his right hand around his tool and started jerking it back and forth. I watched with open eyes, seeing it tingle into super hardness, the crown flaring to its full hooded width and becoming purple with blood. My mouth took on a life of its own, hungry for the splash of sperm. I tried to cover the head of his cock with my lips, but he kept it a few inches away. Finally, I could do no more but to lie back, my head resting on the floor, my mouth wide open, waiting for him to cum. I could already taste the sperm, feel its pungent flavor on my tongue, smell its sharp aroma at the back of my nose. I pictured him spurting, great globs of semen shooting into the air and dropping into my mouth. My throat ached, and I swallowed in anticipation.

His face contorted and his chest tightened and I knew he was close to orgasm. He jerked more and more rapidly, his hand now flying, until he reached a peak. His spine stiffened, his head flew back, and he let out a loud wail as his buttocks contracted and his cock exploded. Thick white jets flew out of the slit in the head and splashed all over me.

The first volley sailed over my head and I moaned in disappointment, but then he began a second series of spurts, and the sticky drops fell on my forehead, onto my chin, and finally on my lips and onto my waiting tongue. As I gobbled the precious fluid, he continued to cum, now dribbling on my throat. I ran my hands over all the places he had splashed and scooped up the sperm with my fingers, and then sucked my fingers dry.

I don't know why I reacted in that way, except that I had made the decision to take the experience on a purely physical level and let my body do what it wanted. I didn't know how I was supposed to act in terms of Jeff's scenario, but we weren't precisely being sensitive to one another's needs at that moment.

For a second, he slumped, and then his eyes brightened. He looked down at me and his face hardened. 'That's the first part, Julie,' he said. 'Shooting all over your face and watching you lick it up, seeing what a *slut* you are. And now to make it official.'

'What are you going to do?' I asked, suddenly worried.

He stood up, yanked me up by one arm, and then lifted me off the floor. He took me into the bathroom, stood me up, and went into the cabinet for a bottle of pills. 'There's something I've learned in pro football,' he said, 'although the coach would kill me if he knew. I've discovered that you can make up for the energy you lose sexually by taking just a little amphetamine, and then there are tablets to help you sleep when you get wound up by nighttime. And these little sleeping pills are for you, Julie, just four of them, so you'll be knocked out enough to not know what's happening.'

I tried to pull back when he twisted one arm behind my back. 'You can take them willingly, or I can shove them down your throat. Which shall it be?'

I had no choice, and I threw the four little pills onto my tongue and washed them down with a glass of water.

Play Time

'What are you going to do to me, Jeff?' I asked, my voice subdued.

'I'm not going to do anything,' he said, 'but I have a friend who is.'

'What?' I asked.

But he wouldn't say another word. He pushed me into the living room and told me to put on some clothes. I found a skirt and blouse and he watched as I put them on. I felt I had reached a base level of erotic despair, for overriding everything else was the certain sense inside me that I wanted more, that I hadn't been satisfied. And I know that that was just what Jeff had intended, to open me up and then turn me loose, thus giving me the liberty I wanted, but with his own peculiar twist.

I sat down and suddenly realized I was exhausted. The week's activities, the emotional and physical drain of the evening, and, I suppose, the sleeping pills, were beginning to work. I fought to keep myself alert, but I knew it would be a vain struggle, so I simply closed my eyes and let myself drift. I don't know how long it took, but within a short time I was foggy, bumping around in that pregnant state between sleep and waking. I heard Jeff making a phone call, but as though from a great distance. And then darkness descended, and I knew no more.

I had odd jumbled dreams, and a vivid flash of seeing two men standing over me doing something to my stomach. I remember disconnected sounds, and jabbing stabs in my belly, but I couldn't hold on to anything that was happening. As happens in such a condition, my thoughts merged with the symbols of the dream life, and the result was an incoherent stream of ideas and sensations which made no sense.

And the next thing I knew, strong sunlight was

shining in my eyes, and Sandy was standing over me.

It took me a minute to clear my head, to figure out where I was, and to remember what had happened the previous night.

'What . . . ?' I said.

'It's OK,' Sandy told me. 'You're in my apartment. Jeff brught you here late last night.'

I tried to sit up, but my body was one huge ache, and it felt as though I had stitches in my belly.

Sandy sat next to me and gently pushed me back.

'Let me guess,' she said. 'He found out about Roger, and you told him you were tired of him, and he went crackers, and worked you over. Right?'

I nodded my head.

'I thought so,' she went on. 'He carried you in here, tossed you on the bed, and said, "Here, another piece of ass to be used by the team".' Sandy bit her lower lip. 'I could swear he had been crying,' she added.

'I didn't know I had got in so deep so fast,' I said between parched lips.

She patted my head. 'But it's over now,' she said. 'You can stay here and rest up, and he'll cool down, and in a few days it will be as though it had never happened.' She paused, looked at me, and said. 'Do you think you still want to stay on as a cheerleader.'

I blinked, and my eyes watered. 'It's strange,' I told her. 'Everything is happening so fast. I don't feel like I'm in control of my life anymore. But it's gripped me. I mean, I feel as though I'm hooked on some kind of weird excitement.'

'I know, kid,' she said. 'It's a lot of money and power and sex and glamor. But let it ride. If you're meant to take the trip all the way, then do it. You'll know when it's time to cut out.'

'There's something,' I said, 'down here.' And reached under the sheet to my stomach.

'It's a bandage,' I exclaimed.

Sandy threw the sheet back and we looked down at my body. 'I saw that when I undressed you,' she said, 'but I thought you knew about it.'

'No.' I replied, suddenly frightened. I looked at Sandy. 'Will you take it off for me?' I asked, 'I'm scared.'

She reached down and gently pulled the tape off the skin, nipping the top edge of pubic hair. She lifted the bandage slowly and then looked down at what was underneath.

'Oh my God!' she said.

'What is it?' I asked.

I glanced down and even though the word was upside down to my vision, I could read it at once. In three-inch blood-red letters, rising up out of my bush, Jeff had had tattooed a single word.

'SLUT' it read.

I looked back up at Sandy, and for an instant we were at the edge of being horrified, but something clicked in our minds, and we turned the whole incident around, grasping it as something we couldn't afford to take seriously.

'Nice,' Sandy said.

'I think that sums it up, don't you?' I replied.

'That Jeff really is a jerk,' she added. 'Everybody knows that the proper spelling for that thing is S-L-I-T.'

'Oh Sandy,' I said, halfway between laughter and tears.

She took my head and held it to her breasts and patted my hair. My arms went around her waist and

Play Time

we hugged each other for a long time. Finally, she moved back, tilted my chin up, and kissed me tenderly on the lips.

'Well,' she said, 'now you have a reputation to live up to. Let's have breakfast and you take a shower and then we'll re-arrange the place so that there's space for both of us here.'

I nodded and watched as she got up to go toward the kitchen. I had stepped on another rung of the ladder, but I wasn't sure whether my direction was up or down.

Six

My father once said, in reference to the ending of his first marriage, that divorce is a form of death. That when a man and a woman form a bond, they create an entity, a gestalt, that is greater than both of them. And when they separate, each of the parts goes back to being itself; but the other thing, the living relationship, dies.

I suppose I felt that about what happened with Jeff, although we had had so relatively little with each other. After that night, I went about more than a little subdued. Yet, I felt lucky, for if we had continued and gone on to live with one another, that embryonic bond that had already formed between us would have developed into a tie that might not have been sundered short of murder, either physical or psychological.

But time worked its melancholy process, replacing pain with poignancy, poignancy with forgetfulness, and forgetfulness with new direction. The summer passed quickly, and I rarely saw Jeff except for fleeting moments on the field. During the day I went dutifully through my practice sessions, and at night I took up the erotic games which constituted the *leitmotif* of the cheerleaders' existence. Just before the first game of the season, I had been fucked by more than twenty of the players, in addition to several of the executive staff.

But the two who attracted me most strongly remained distant. Jack, the volcanically virile trainer, came to take a fatherly attitude toward me that was strangely disturbing and made me feel vulnerable. Partly because I was goaded by the other girls and partly because I was curious, I set a collision course with him, and finally managed to be lying on the couch in the dressing room wearing nothing but a smile when he barged in. It was almost evening, and no one else was around, and I thought that he would take the opportunity to do his much-vaunted number.

But he seemed totally impassive, and glanced at my body without desire or curiosity. Rather, he closed the door behind him, took a chair, and slid it under him, the back facing me so he could rest his chin on the top supporting rung.

'I know what you're trying to do,' he said, his gravelly voice sounding almost tender. 'But I'm not interested. You've been infected with this sickness, and you won't rest until you've fucked every man in sight, at least everyone except those rare few who still hold the marriage vows sacred. But I don't think that's really you. It looks like some sort of game.' I must have shown some consternation on my face for he hurriedly added, 'And I don't disapprove. I mean, you're doing what you want to, or need to. But it's just that when you get it all out of your system, or into your system, whichever it is, you won't end up like Sandy and the others. They're good people, and I like them, but they're basically whores.'

'And I'm just a slut,' I said, thrusting out my belly so the tattoo surged toward him.

'That's what you tell yourself. And . . . look, it's not my place to say these things, but since you offered yourself to me, I feel I should tell you what's on my mind. I hope you work it all out without damaging yourself, and someday find someone you can love.'

'Thanks for the advice, *Dad*,' I snarled, trying to sound biting, but actually I was close to tears.

He smiled, and stood to go. 'OK,' he said. 'That's all I have to say.' He turned and walked to the door, but before going out he added, 'But if any of those jokers gives you any trouble, or tries to beat up on you, let me know, and I'll crack a few skulls.'

After he left I almost succumbed to the sadness he had brought to the surface, but I bit my lip and determined that I would not let myself be washed down that particular stream. I hurled myself into an opposing mood, and went to the telephone to call Nick Johnston, a second-string tackle who had been trying to set up a scene with me and some of his friends. I told him I would be over that night, and that he could invite whomever he liked.

I showered, dressed, and kept talking to myself to maintain my sense of aggression and control. I was riding too high over too dangerous a ground to allow myself to slip. I had no one to catch me. I put on my tightest pair of shorts and a halter, piled into the Kharmann-Gia I had already made two payments on, and drove to Nick's apartment.

Waiting with him were Sal Tancredi and Joey Washington, both guards. Nick stood almost six feet eight inches tall, and weighed nearly two hundred and seventy pounds. Each of the other men was about six feet tall, but they must have been nearly three hundred pounds apiece. They all stood up as

Play Time

I entered, and I was staggered by what I had agreed to take on. I felt frail and incredibly tiny when faced by almost a ton of muscle and bone coupled with the coiled fury each had had trained into his body. I could see their eyes glisten as they raked my thighs and breasts with hot glances. And as I walked past them I knew they were devouring the back of my body, watching the way my ass swayed and shook, cupped tightly in the clinging shorts.

There was little point in extended preliminaries, since we all knew why we were there. The word was out that I was a hot bitch, a hungry twat. And, of course, my tattoo had made me nearly legendary. Sandy told me that the locker room talk had evaluated me as a wild cunt, who would take cock in the ass, down the throat, between the tits, in the hands, and was ready to wriggle, roll, grovel, beg and suck anything from tongues to assholes.

We sat around for fifteen or twenty minutes, drinking quickly, and killing a fifth of vodka in no time at all. Nick and Sal sat on either side of me on the couch, while Joey sat cross-legged on the floor in front of me, his eyes rarely leaving my crotch. I was aware of the strange power that is inherent in a woman, or how I could mesmerize and hold captive these three neo-Neanderthals with the single promise of letting them stuff my holes with their rampaging cocks.

The vibrations in the room got thicker and heavier, and it became difficult to talk. Even the fact that we were maintaining the pretense of polite company was highly electrifying, introducing a charged smuttiness into every word and gesture. My cunt went turgid and my ass seemed to melt. A deep lethargy stole over me and I let myself sink into the delicious space

Play Time

of surrender, knowing that they would take control, and I would need to do nothing but lie back and let them fill me with their extravagant energy. I wondered whether this was technically an act of vampirism on my part.

I slid down on the seat and rested my head against the back, and then, boldly, closed my eyes. The following few seconds of silence was filled with intimations of movement, and I could almost hear them nodding to one another, congratulating themselves on my being precisely what they had heard I was, an open cunt, ready to spread my legs at the merest invitation.

Then, abruptly, hands were on my tits and on my thighs. A sea of flesh broke over me, lips on mine, fingers tugging at my clothing. A tongue attacked my nipples as my shirt was raised over my head, and coarse knuckles pressed into my pussy as my shorts were tugged down my legs. I moaned and let myself sink into the vortex which had been formed by my self-abandonment.

'Wow, she's really a slut,' said one of the men, 'look at her.'

'Yes,' I thought, 'look at me. Watch me writhe and claw the air. See my tits shake and my nipples wrinkle. Observe how my legs kick and how my cunt spreads. See my mouth purse and my tongue lick the air. Watch me go wild and thrash around on the floor. Do you want more? Let me turn over and you can feast your eyes on my lovely ass, that simple and mysterious shape which holds more power over a man than the wealth of the world. Is that enough? Does it drive you mad? Do you want to touch this wanton body? Run your fingers into my hot wet slit? Slide your tongues into my asshole? Pinch my nipples? Listen to me moan. Know that you can do whatever you want with me and let that thought inflame you. Are your cocks throbbing? Then put them where it will feel good. Bury them in my gaping pussy. Thrust them rudely and slowly into my asshole. Rub them on my tits. Cram them in my mouth. What else? Do you want to sit on my face? Do you want to whip me? Do it! Do all of it!'

As had so often happened during sex, I could find no way this time to make any connection between my feeling of abandonment and the actual abandonment of my behaviour. Paradoxically, although I was experiencing inside myself the same thing that was going on outside myself, it was as though I had been split into two separate people, unable to communicate with one another. I imagine the cause lay in my inability to speak my feelings, and since works are the bridge between the interior and exterior life, when they are blocked a chasm opens in the person.

'Didn't I tell you?' Nick replied. 'She loves it, she'll do anything.'

'That's me they're talking about,' I said to myself.

They then proceeded to use me as the fulfillment of their fantasies and projections. It's almost impossible to describe how small I felt as they tossed me around and bent me into all sorts of lewd positions, holding me upside down and moving my legs to every conceivable angle so that my cunt would twist and gape and perform for their avid eyes. They threw me about as though I were a rag doll, and at one point two of them lifted me off the ground, bent me double with my forehead touching my shinbones, forcing my ass to its deepest curve, and then ran across the room with me, as though I were a battering ram. At the far end stood Sal, his cock stiff and pointed, and Nick and Joey swung me toward him and with a single careful thrust impaled me on his rock-hard rod.

I yelled out loud as the huge shaft burst inside me, but the two men holding me shook me up and down, spun me over, and whacked me again and again against Sal's throbbing cock, giving it a massage with my ragged hole. It was obvious that the three of them were fixated at a level of adolescent homosexual horseplay, and didn't have the faintest idea of how to relate to a woman except as a surrogate hand to whack off with. And lacking the simple decency to do it to one another, they sought out female bodies to hide behind.

I suppose I got too far lost in my head because the boys began to grumble that I had become too passive in my body. The slightest hint that I was not flinging myself mindlessly into the fray would prove too threatening to their privacy, so they began to whip up a frenzy.

I was hurled onto the rug and Nick threw himself heavily onto my shoulders, pinning them with his knees, and grinding his buttocks down on my face.

'Lick it,' he ordered, bringing his asshole to my lips. I curled up my tongue and slid it into the right puckered opening.

One of the other men seized my legs and pulled them high and wide, forcing my cunt open, while the third knelt at my parted pussy. I tried to yell as he tore into the tender lips, licking and sucking. He blew into the hole filling it with air and sending me into paroxysms of strained pleasure, and then sucked out noisily, draining me of the injected air and the juices that had started to flow despite myself. But whenever I opened my mouth to shout, Nick pressed down harder, and I could do nothing but glue my lips to his asshole and suck voraciously, all the while slipping my tongue rapidly in and out.

The mouth at my cunt withdrew, leaving my twat sore and trembling, but what followed made that little more than foreplay.

'Let me do it,' I heard Joey say, and then felt a pressure against the outside of my cunt. For a second I didn't know what it was, but then the sensations became unmistakeable: fingers rolled into a fist were pushing slowly against my tiny opening.

'Shove it up her snatch,' Nick said, 'shove that fist all the way up that pretty little pussy.'

I didn't think I would be able to stretch enough, but I had no choice. With all their weight and power holding me down, I was no more able to move than if a ten-ton truck had fallen on me. Nick pulled my legs more widely apart, almost cracking the tendons, and Sal squashed my face with his ass, while Joey stuffed my slit with his huge hand.

Suddenly, I thought, 'Oh my God, I can't take it.' But at that moment I heard Joey exclaim, 'Did it, I did it. Look at it. My fist is all the way up her snatch. Look at that pussy spread.'

'Man,' said Nick, 'look at the way those lips grip your wrist.'

'Fuck her with it,' Sal said, 'fist-fuck her good'.

And with that Joey started to rotate his wrist, twisting his fist around inside me.

My legs were released and I immediately tried to close my thighs, but that only had the effect of trapping the fist more tightly inside me, and I could feel its powerful bulk more strongly. Free to move my body, I began to thrash about, at first trying to wriggle away from the pressure of that hand, but very soon I realized that I was also trying to stuff it more deeply inside me. The pressure was still very keen, but now that I had no fear of being torn, I could let the underlying pleasure come to the surface, and that was more than incidental. Having a three-hundred pound man shove his hand into my cunt and fuck my pussy with harsh strokes and twists was no mean erotic experience.

I began to grind my hips and thrust my pelvis up, fucking the hand that had been fucking me. I brought my own hands up to spread the cheeks that were pressed on my face, and sucked Sal's asshole rapturously as I worked toward climax on Joey's arm. Nick started in on my tits, pinching the nipples and sucking the globes into his mouth, using his teeth to punctuate the swirls of his tongue. And before I knew it, I had stopped thinking about what I was doing and what it meant and if it was some form of escape or degeneracy, and just let myself be worked over by three brutes, as I flung my mouth and ass and pussy and tits into full overdrive, retrieving my reputation as the dirtiest cheerleader on the team.

Then, abruptly, Nick pulled his hand out, the fist escaping with a loud plop. Moaning, gasping, spluttering, I turned onto my side. More than anything, I had to have that thing between my legs again. His pulling out had left my hole more aware of its emptiness than it had ever been. My cunt felt as though it had been pulled inside out and was now lying like a punctured balloon against my thighs.

'Oooh,' I moaned.

'She wants more,' Nick said.

'Let me do her,' Joey hissed.

'Unngh,' I cried as I pushed my hips off the floor and thrust my cunt into the air.

'Oh, yeah, baby,' Joey whispered, 'I'm going to give it to you, going to get right up that dripping pussy.'

He put his balled fist against my cunt and pressed, and this time I thrust against it, engulfing it in a single motion.

'Ahhh,' I sighed as my cunt was once again stuffed far past its usual capacity.

'Look at her,' Sal said. 'Ain't she beautiful!'

'Fuck it,' Joey said, 'fuck my fist you hot bitch. Come on, push that pretty pussy all over my hand.'

Their words enflamed me and I started to squeeze my ass tight and pump my hips back and forth, doing a fucking motion against the force of his arm.

Then Sal turned me over and bent me in two so that my cunt curved under and my ass turned up. And while Joey ground his fist in and out and around, massaging my cunt, and making me scratch the rug in an ecstasy of ravishment, Sal lowered his bulk down, brought his cock between my cheeks, and sank it slowly into my asshole. I was almost paralyzed with sensation, being stuffed beyond my wildest dreams. And Nick completed the picture by lifting my head by the hair and then letting it fall, having placed his cock below my mouth so that as my face came forward, the stiff flesh staff would slide between my lips.

They fucked me like that for more than three hours, taking turns filling my holes, using their cocks and hands and feet, placing me in whatever positions they wanted, throwing me around whenever they needed. And I variously loathed myself, or lost myself in orgasmic frenzy, or became indifferent to the process. But by the time they were finished, I could not stand up, and was barely able to raise an

Play Time

arm or keep my head erect. They had to dress me, and drive me back to Sandy's and my apartment. But by the time we had gone cross town they were horny again, and I had to blow each of them as they sat in the car, only their zippers open, their cocks erupting in my mouth one after the other, until my throat was clogged with sperm. Knowing they might not have me again, they took every last opportunity to feel me up, fingering my asshole and twiddling my pussy and kneading my tits as I sucked their cocks.

But finally, there was nothing left, and I dragged myself off to bed, grateful that the next day was a vacation, part of a three-day rest before the team was to play its first game on the road, in Denver.

By this time, I had come to feel pretty much at home with the idea of being part of the team, and was even learning a lot about the game by hearing different plays and kinds of strategy discussed all the time. But it wasn't until that first crisp autumn afternoon in the Denver stadium that the true excitement of the game struck me. Up to then, I had been involved in practice and preparation, not realizing that that was just a pale shadow of the real thing, both for the team and for the cheerleaders.

The sky was achingly blue and the temperature a zippy fifty degrees. The other three women and myself strutted up and down the sidelines, and drew more than a fair share of whistles and applause. I could even see some men signalling to me frantically, and I knew that I could make more than a small addition to my salary by being available to affluent men who got overly horny during a game. Sandy told me she had put away more than ten thousand dollars the previous year by judicious appointments with admirers in the stands. But I was too thrilled to think in those terms that day, and was having a ball flaunting my tits and showing my ass and causing an untold number of erective thoughts in the stadium.

Then the teams came charging out of their dugouts, and the crowd exploded, a deep surging roar that set my ears ringing. The sound swelled like thundering surf, and I rode down its foaming crest like a joyous surfer, letting it enter me until I could no longer distinguish the pounding of my heart or the throbbing of my pulse. I lept high in the air and out of the corner of my eye saw Sandy and Irene and Marian rising with me, their arms high and their legs bent at the knees, heels pressed into their buttocks. I grinned widely and let out a shout at the top of my lungs.

The four of us jumped again and again until I was breathing hard, and then we ran in patterns around one another, going through the routines we had so diligently practiced for three months, throwing up banners and doing bumps and grinds to the music of the team band. It seemed the most happy moment of my life, a period in which I stood totally out of myself, experiencing the true meaning of the word ecstasy. And when the two teams lined up for the kickoff, I looked at the Seattle lineup and my cunt throbbed as I realized that seven of the eleven men now standing there resplendent in muscle and uniform and determination had been inside me, that I had circled their backs with my arms, bit their chests, and sucked their cocks into my mouth and pussy. The whistle blew, the line moved forward, and the ball sailed high into the air.

From that instant on, all was pandemonium. I didn't have a moment's rest, but spent the time urging the crowd to cheer the team on, with Sandy, our captain, calling the routines which were appropriate to different situations. We appealed for touchdowns, we implored them to hold the line and block the kick. And in general exhausted ourselves, throwing our bodies into the struggle as heavily in our way as the men were going in theirs. And always, behind us and in front of us and inside us was the sound, the perpetual roar, the song of animal excitement. The afternoon was like a long vigorous fuck, and when the final gun went off, with Seattle winning seventeen to six, I lept once more into the air and screamed in victory.

I must have been overly carried away by the moment because when I came down, I landed on the edge of my right foot and felt my ankle turn under me. A sharp stab of pain shot up my leg, and I almost fainted, my face going chalk white and beads of perspiration breaking out on my forehead. I lay on the ground writhing in agony, and to my surprise, the first one to reach me was Tony.

Something of a flurry of people developed around us, but he scooped me up in his arms and walked directly toward the dugout, went down the stairs and into the cheerleaders' dressing room without hesitation. I was amazed at how strong he was and realized that although he was at least six feet tall, his slenderness made him seem puny in relation to the physical monsters on the team, especially when they had all their gear on.

He put me down on the couch and went over to close and lock the door, telling the people who had followed us that I would be better off without a crowd of rubbernecks making me nervous. I was still a bit dazed and watched the whole scene as though through a fog. When the door was shut, he turned toward me and his eyes were blazing with anger.

'That was the dumbest thing I have ever seen,' he shouted.

I couldn't believe my ears. I had thought he had taken me in to give me sympathy and instead he was pouring hostility on my head. I tried to prop myself up on my elbows to answer him, but the sudden shift caused the excruciating pain to pierce my leg again and I had to lie back down.

'How many times have I told you to be especially careful about how you land after a high leap? What were you doing all summer, dozing? Or have you had so many cocks down your throat that it's affected your hearing?'

My jaw dropped open in astonishment. Ignoring the pain, I sat up, and with tears brimming at the corners of my eyes I answered him, 'Who the hell do you think you are?' I began. 'It's none of your goddamned business what I do during my free time. And I might have a broken ankle, and you're standing there giving me lectures!'

'Your ankle isn't broken,' he shot back.

'How do you know?' I asked, now almost sobbing openly from pain and chagrin.

'I'm in the business,' he said. But as though relenting, he came over, took the ankle in his hands, pressed it, turned it back and forth, bringing me close to fainting again. 'We'll have it x-rayed,' he went on, 'but I'll stake my reputation on the fact that it's not broken.'

'Well, why did you bring me here?' I shrieked as he dropped my foot unceremoniously on the couch. 'To give me more pain and deliver your opinions on my life?'

'I brought you here because I'm responsible for

you, for all the cheerleaders. And because I was pissed off at your stupid stunt, and wanted to tell you that before everybody began showering you with sympathy.'

'And you can't be bothered with any of that, can you? You . . . you . . . eunuch.'

I hadn't intended to say that but I suppose that his cavalier attitude and rough treatment, coupled with his indifference to my come-ons during the summer, had built up a reservoir of resentment.

'What's going on in there?' said a voice from the other side of the door. 'Open up.'

'Fuck off!' Tony shouted.

He turned back to me. 'Eunuch,' he said. 'Why? Because I haven't fucked you? Because I haven't volunteered to stand in line to take sloppy seconds and fifths and twentieths? I have no interest in the meaningless.'

I wanted to scream, to protest, to fight, but the pain kept pulling me toward it, raping my attention. And his words were delivered with such cold precision that they cut down all my resistance. And on top of all that, he was right about my turning my ankle being a dumb stunt. He had warned us against that at least a few hundred times. I felt utterly defeated and simply turned my face to the back of the couch and began to cry, letting all my unhappiness rise to the surface and wash over me.

I must have wept for several minutes, and when I finished I felt drained and purged. I looked back toward Tony, a little embarrassed at having had him see me that way, but to my astonishment he was smoking a cigarette and staring off toward the far wall. From behind the door I could hear voices, one man saying, 'What the fuck are they doing in there?'

and another answering. 'What else does that chick ever do man? It's probably a new kick, fucking with a broken ankle.'

I was aware that Tony was hearing the conversation also, and our minds met in that realization and as though on cue he turned to look at me. His eyes were sad, almost moist.

'What a waste, Julie,' he said in a low trembling voice. 'You are so beautiful, so intelligent, so filled with life, and look at how you throw it away. And now you weep over spilled milk. What's the point?'

'I'm working my life out in my own way,' I said, and was astonished to hear the tone of my voice. He was a man I had had no contact with outside of our practice sessions, and suddenly I was speaking to him seriously and intimately, without anger or bravado, but as one speaks to a friend or lover. 'You don't know me, how can you say the things you do?'

'You don't know what I know,' he said. 'Just because I don't say anything or act out my impulses doesn't mean I don't observe and perceive and understand. I know you more deeply than you realize, and I feel things for you which would surprise you.'

My head swam. It sounded as though he were on the verge of a declaration of love, this strange introverted man whom the other women presented to me as a challenge to our powers of seduction, and whom I tried from time to time to lure from his isolation. And I couldn't figure out where his words were coming from.

'Of course I noticed you when you arrived,' he went on. 'And when I first looked into your eyes, something happened to me, something that both excited and frightened me. I knew you were Jeff's girl, but that didn't matter, not until he began to show home movies in the locker room. And even then I wasn't disturbed too much, because it was not my place to translate your actions into my terms. But then it was Roger, and then Steve, and then Al, and now so many I can't keep count. And yesterday I was treated to the full detailed history of your debauch with Nick and his friends. And through all this, the feeling persisted, and grew, and at one point I knew that I wanted to take you into my arms and hold you and kiss you and tell you that I loved you, because I understood you.'

'Oh, Tony,' I breathed, overwhelmed by his torrent of feeling. And unconsciously I shifted my weight, let my legs fall open, and thrust my breasts forward in invitation.

But he merely curled his lip. 'What does that gesture mean anymore?' he said. 'You'd respond the same way with an orangutan. Your pussy is worthless. You've given it away too many times. And how can I kiss you, when I know you've pressed your lips against every cock and asshole that's been offered?'

My eyes must have shown bewilderment, because he went on, 'Oh, I'm not a puritan. I don't care about the specifics. It's just that you're so goddamned indiscriminate, so tasteless, so . . . *vulgar*.' He took one step toward me and then stopped. The sudden movement had the effect of catapulting him out of the two-dimensional sheet in which I had been viewing the world and into a three-dimensional *thereness* which stunned me. He ceased being an image, and became a person, someone *other*, and that entity was thrust into my self-involved universe. I suddenly realized – I'm almost embarrassed to say the word – how handsome he was. Not in a movie star sense, but in his extraordinary maleness. And with that came the understanding that he had been training me for three months, and that I had totally underestimated how deep our relationship actually was. I was overcome with a deep sense of loss.

'Don't you see?' he went on. 'It's not that I don't desire you, or haven't desired Sandy or any of the others. But that I hold desire to be so precious that I can't abide its being made coarse and cheap.'

My gaze faltered and fell down the length of his body. To my amazement I saw that his cock was bulging in his pants. 'Oh, Tony,' I said again.

He put his hand on his cock and smiled bitterly. 'This?' he said. 'There's more to it than that, Julie.'

Once more there was a pounding on the door, and this time Tony went over and opened it up. The team doctor was standing there, along with Sandy and the other cheerleaders and a few members of the team. They all rushed in at once, all speaking, all solicitous, and in a moment I was being comforted and examined and made a fuss over. But I didn't want any of them, I wanted Tony. I tried to call to him but he was already gone, and I bit my lip as I fell back on the couch.

'Does it hurt, baby?' Sandy asked.

And for the second time that day I started to cry. 'Yes, it hurts,' I said, holding her hand, but I wasn't referring just to my ankle, but also to a deep ache in my heart.

That night I dreamt of Tony. He stood before me naked and I knelt in front of him, his erect cock close to my lips. It began to throb, and he started to cum. But instead of sperm, hot scalding tears cascaded from its single blind eye.

Seven

The ankle wasn't broken, but before I was able to use it again, I had missed the following week's game. I began to understand the significance of what Roger had told me about the cohesiveness of the team; it was like being part of a large family. I was pampered, sent flowers, and reassured by everyone from the President to the water boy. I spent ten days back in Sandy's and my apartment, recuperating, and when I was completely healed flew from there to Los Angeles to meet the team for their third game. They had won their second match and had become the sportswriters' favorites to take first place in the league and go into the superbowl with the champions of the Eastern Division.

During the time I was laid up I had plenty of opportunity to think about my life and where it was heading. The encounter with Tony had proved to be profoundly unsettling especially since I received no word from him since. My feelings about him remained formless. I had always thought him attractive, but only as one of my potential sexual conquests. Now that he had revealed the deeper level to our relationship, one which I hadn't even been aware of, I didn't know how to think about him. It was difficult to differentiate guilt from desire, and I wasn't sure how much of what was troubling me was from my own sense of self or from the images he had imposed on me.

One afternoon, I stood for some time in front of a full-length mirror, examining myself to find what it might be in me that Tony had responded to. It was a foolish exercise, and yet what is time for but to experiment with? 'What is it, Julie?' I said to my reflection. 'You're obviously pretty and have a sexy body and a good mind, but you're not that much different from a thousand other women who surrounded you on campus. Jeff certainly had no trouble finding anyone he wanted to go to bed with him, yet why was he so taken with you? And Tony is turning out to be an extraordinary man who has at least three beautiful women chasing him; what makes him find you so special?'

I lifted my tits and pushed them forward, watching them swell, the smooth white skin bulging around my dark pointed nipples. 'Is it these? These sacs of fatty tissue?' I brought my hands down to my cunt and parted the lips, exposing the pink interior. 'Or this? This tiny wrinkled slit?' Spinning around I tilted my ass up and saw it in the glass, the twin round globes iridescent around the dark soft crack. 'Or this? Evolution's practical joke?' I walked up to the mirror and pressed my lips against it, licking the glass with my tongue, making pools of mist with my breath. 'Or is it my mouth they desire?'

I stepped back in consternation. None of that made any sense. Those were things that any woman possessed, some in a more aesthetically gratifying way than others, but on that level we were all interchangeable. Was it then some quality? Many of the men had commented on my wildness, my capacity for lustful frenzy. That had turned Jeff on, but Tony had relegated it to the category of the incidental. I remembered his saying that it had no importance if it became the plaything of every man who came by.

No, there was something that was more than the sum of my parts, and I could only call it my uniqueness, my individuality, my me-ness. In the way that the mirror could not see itself, so I could not be aware of that essential aspect which was so utterly myself that I must remain blind to it. Only another could see me in that space, and it was precisely the person who did perceive who truly loved. For he or she then called an entity out of its condition of formlessness, who, in a very real sense, created a conscious human being where before there had only been an instinctive functioning.

This train of thought brought to mind passages from various texts I had studied in my philosophy and psychology classes, and for the first time I realized that I might have done myself real damage by leaving school. While I believed that the experience I was gaining on the team was invaluable, I sensed that I could derive more benefit from it if I had the tools of analysis to assist me, and the writings of people who had pondered life deeply to guide me.

As though we were in telepathic communication, my father sent me a letter which I received the very afternoon of the day I stood wondering about my life before the mirror. I had written him about my quitting school and becoming a cheerleader, and had mentioned Jeff, speaking about him as a lover, but had not gone into any details concerning my extraordinary sexual activity. His note was brief and, although acid in tone, comforting.

'Dear Julie,' he wrote, 'asininity is a prerogative of the young. So is a sense of independence. Guard against early marriage, pregnancy, and venereal disease. Your mother, as usual, finds your vicissitudes too boring to comment on. Should you desire to return to the academic structure after this complex fling, we will honor our pledge to see you financially through your Master's. I have never offered you the false security of assuming that my wisdom is any greater than yours. I have simply observed more patterns than you, that's all. Should you falter, you will always have a refuge here. We are not effusive, as you know, but we care deeply for your welfare. Your brother has gone mad, but since he is expressing his insanity in a socially acceptable format, he is enjoying himself immensely. I find some slight vicarious titillation in imagining the orgies you must be attending. Remember that intelligence is the highest good, and the rarest accomplishment. Affectionately, Carl. P.S. We shall watch the next Seattle game on television to see how well you have learned to leap.'

My period of isolation and the knowledge that my family, if they did not precisely approve, continued to accept me as a daughter and would sustain me if things got too rough, restored my sense of well-being. I decided to put the incident with Tony on a shelf at the back of my mind. He seemed to show no inclination to follow up and I wasn't going to lay myself open to him in any way. I felt healthy and sane and looked forward to the further developments of the season. I didn't know what the future held, and that was exactly what I found so exciting. As far as the notion that I was becoming the slut that Jeff had branded me, I was ready to pursue that to its final conclusion. Already it was apparent that this was a phase, and I knew that unless I cycled through it completely, I would regret my timidity for the rest of my life.

In short, I had integrated all that had happened up to that point, and was ready for more action. I had no way of knowing what that would be, and if I had had any suspicion of what lay in store I might not have made my decision so jauntily. As with so many things in life, I began a new round with enough renewed vitality and sense of integrity to bring about an explosive erotic evening. So delightful was it that it made me too sure of myself, of my ability to control the forces which were already swirling about my feet.

The team was met by a particularly tough Los Angeles squad, and the ensuing game was punctuated with penalties and fistfights. There were a few fireworks as the players settled down to a grueling ground game, each side rarely able to even churn out a first down. That, coupled with my sense of pleasure in being in Los Angeles again, plus the welcome-back attitude on the part of everyone on the team, catapulted me into an inspired cheerleader performance. I threw my heart into my movements and shouts. And when, with four minutes left to play, our quarterback called for a kick from our thirty yard line and instead uncorked a surprise pass to Jeff, the crowd went wild, lifting me up with them. Los Angeles was taken completely off balance by the fake kick, and when Jeff caught the ball midfield, there wasn't another man near him. I screamed myself hoarse as he hit his stride and began speeding downfield, bounding over the earth like some mythical steed. And it was with a thunderous roar in my ears that I watched him cross the goal line with what proved to be the winning touchdown.

Play Time

The final few minutes involved perfunctory play as a re-charged Seattle defensive team came in to hold Los Angeles to no gain. The gun went off as three of our linebackers swarmed all over the opposing quarterback and smashed him into the ground with the ball still in his hand. Since I had been fucked by each of the men in that play I felt an especially personal thrill in the victory.

My ebullience was augmented when, as I was coming out of the dressing room after changing, I was approached by Larry Plains, the fullback, a gorgeous black with enormous shoulders and a waist almost as narrow as mine. He was called swivel-hips because of his ability to spin away from would-be tacklers, and I had had my eye on him for some time. Although I was not consciously prejudiced, there was still that part of me which wondered if and how a black man would be different in bed. And from the look in his eyes, I figured I was about to soon find out.

But he invited me to Frank Williams' house, to have dinner with Frank and his wife and three other couples. Frank was the star quarterback who risked so much calling the fake kick deep in his own territory, and as far as I knew he didn't fuck around at all. For an instant I wondered why Larry was inviting me to what appeared to be a staid evening, but decided that he might want to spend some time with me socially before fucking me, and that was enough of an oddity to intrigue me.

Frank and his wife had apartments in a number of cities so they could be, as Laura Williams explained, 'at home wherever we go.' Their place was surprisingly chic for what I imagined was a square couple. The dining room was sparse, and we ate out of bucketsful of Kentucky Fried Chicken, washing it down with a good red wine. The other couples were relatively strange to me, all the men forming that small percentage of the team which seemed to be, if not happily then at least, securely married. I was on nodding acquaintance with all of them, but had never met their wives.

The meal went cheerfully, with everyone recounting anecdotes of the day's play. At one point Larry slipped his hand under the table and stroked my thigh, and I breathed a bit easier with the feeling of being on familiar ground. After Tony, a man who wanted nothing more complicated that to slide his hard cock into my randy gap provided welcome relief.

After eating we went into the living room, which proved a real surprise. There was nothing in it but deep pile rug and large throw pillows. The lights were so low that it was difficult to make out another person's features at a distance of more than five feet. Music came from somewhere, a drum recording which sounded like Olatunji underwater. Given the texture of my life, I don't know how I could have missed what was happening, but so strong is the power of pre-conception that with my notion of these people as married squares I was completely blind to the purpose of the evening.

I sat on one of the pillows, resigned to another hour or so of chatter, when Melanie, the wife of Harvey Engram, sashayed to the middle of the room and began doing a slow bump and grind. For an instant I didn't perceive it as anything but a bit of spontaneous dancing, but in a few seconds her movements began to be more sharply defined. Her broad ass, caught in a tight velour dress, circled suggestively, while her shoulders shook back and forth, causing her full-bellied breasts to sway, I guess I still didn't understand until she brought her hands up and slowly peeled the dress off her shoulders, letting it slide down her sides. And before I could grasp the fact that she was stripping, her creamy and pink-tipped tits were totally revealed.

'Bravo,' shouted Jim Reynolds, one of the other players.

I half-turned toward Larry, to confirm the suspicion that had formed in my mind, but I couldn't tear my eyes away from Melanie, who had now eased the dress down her thighs, showing the full bristling bush which covered her thick-lipped twat.

'What's the matter, Julie?' Frank called out, 'your eyes are popping out of your head. You act as though you'd never been to a party before.'

'But, all you people are . . . *married*,' I said, the last word slipping out before I realized how foolish it sounded.

The laughter that met my remark, however, was good-natured, and Larry reached over and put his arm around me. 'Honey, these people are all swingers,' he said. 'I thought you knew that.' He looked at me for a moment and then went on, 'You didn't think I was inviting you to just a dinner party, did you?'

I nodded. 'I'm afraid I did,' I said.

'Well, hell,' Larry sang out. 'I'm flat-out flattered!'

And once again the room rang with laughter. By now the men had begun to remove their shirts and unhook their belts, while the other women were shrugging themselves clear of their dresses.

'It's OK, isn't it?' Larry said in a low voice. 'I mean, I assumed that you would be into it.'

'You mean, with my reputation?' I replied a bit acerbically.

But I didn't give him a chance to continue, wanting to get the flow of the event moving. I had, of course, heard of the phenomenon of swinging, but had never given it any detailed thought, and now I was curious to see how these couples operated in their effort to have their cake and eat it too.

'It's OK, Larry,' I said. 'I feel like I've just been given a surprise party.'

To underline my words I pulled my blouse up over my head and flung it to one side, sitting there with my bare tits pointing out toward Larry's gleaming eyes. I saw him form the word 'beautiful' soundlessly with his lips before he leaned forward and cupped each of my breasts in his two powerful hands. I looked down and caught my breath to see the stunning contrast of his jet black skin against my pale white flesh. The visual impact was even more thrilling than the sensations caused by his fingers rubbing gently over my nipples.

I must have become lost in reverie because I didn't notice that the others had all gathered in front of me, and I looked up to see eight naked men and women lying and sitting all around Larry watching him stroke my breasts. I think I may have blushed, for the moment was quite stark.

'Can we see it?' said Laura Williams.

'See it?' I repeated.

'The tattoo,' she said, 'We've heard so much about the tattoo.'

'Fuck the tattoo,' said Jim Reynolds, 'I want to see that young pussy.'

'Don't be crude,' said his wife Karen, admonishing him as she might a schoolboy.

I began to reply but before I could say a word a dozen hands were at my waist, unhooking the button and pulling the zipper down and finally snaking the pants off my legs. They all pressed in close to see, and I heard a chorus of muted oohs and aahs as they examined the scarlet stigma rising like a flame out of my pubic hair. Someone whose hands had been fingering the letters ran his hands lower down and began tickling the edges of my cunt lips, causing me to squirm. But Larry dove in and pushed them all aside.

'My date,' he said imperiously, 'and I get firsts.'

He had undressed and his body was even more commanding naked than it had been even with full gear. I had seen him run many times and wondered how it would feel to hold those churning hips in my hands as his cock plunged in and out of my pussy. In the dim light he looked like a smoke demon and I lay back almost in awe as he knelt between my thighs.

'We can help, can't we?' said Susie December, the wife of the fifth man there.

'Just leave me her snatch and you can do what you want with the rest,' Larry said.

Laura Williams lay down next to me and began caressing one of my breasts, her soft hand stroking the firm flesh gently. 'Don't feel picked on,' she whispered after sliding her tongue in my ear sending shivers down my spine, 'it's just that we've been together a hundred times and you're the new girl in town. So naturally everybody wants a taste of you first.'

They moved around me like a well-rehearsed theatrical group. Harvey put his cock in my right hand

Play Time

and Tom December put his cock in my left hand. Jim knelt by my head and slipped his half-erect cock between my lips. One of the other women began to suck my other breast, and the others positioned themselves in various spots, so that my belly was sucked and my ass fondled. Before long I was covered with attention, my entire body subject to one or another form of touch.

At first it wasn't specifically exciting, partially because everyone was so methodical and matter-of-fact, but the sheer volume of flesh and level of energy wasn't too long in having an effect, and in short order I was beginning to lose my mundane sense of self to an identification with the erotic current, a tingling warmth which brought my skin to life and slowly burned more deeply into my insides. My breath came more quickly and Jim's cock swelled to full erection and he pumped it back and forth slowly into my mouth. I locked it with my tongue, wetting it, making slobbering noises, as with each hand I stroked the thick rods that had grown stiff with my fondling.

A finger went into my ass and I began to squirm, suddenly catching on to the erotic mood like a person climbing aboard a bicycle after many years and suddenly remembering perfectly how to ride. Tony's treatment of me and the ten-day period of solitude had removed me from a sense of sex, and now, with a grateful rush, I was recapturing it.

'Get the bitch hot,' Larry whispered. 'Get her good and wet and hot.'

'The bitch,' I thought to myself. 'There it is again. That's all I am to him, to these people.' And almost simultaneously with that idea, another voice popped into my head. 'This is no time to get finicky,' it said.

'You're here to enjoy a friendly orgy. Be a hot little cunt and enjoy it.'

I suppose I might have continued the argument with myself, but my body had a different perspective. It was going on without any need for approval from the mind. My legs were thrashing and my nipples getting hard and my cunt starting to drip. Everywhere there were hands or mouths or cocks or tits pressed on me. I was awash in a sea of sensuality, and my hungry flesh was drinking it in.

'What a sweet pussy,' Frank hissed. 'Look at that, Laura, isn't it pretty.'

'I can hardly wait for you to fuck her,' Laura replied. 'And after you cum I'm going to eat your sperm right out of her tight little snatch.'

It seemed odd to hear a husband and wife talk like that, but I suspected it was healthier in its way than most of what goes on between conventional couples. By this time I was highly enflamed, twisting my hips and thrusting my pelvis out. Everything was being touched except my cunt, and I was getting delirious with desire. Which is what I guess Larry wanted.

'That's it, baby,' he said, 'throw that pussy up in the air. Come on, give it here, push it out. Beg with it, Julie. I want to see your pussy beg for my cock.'

I reached higher with my cunt, spread my legs wider, tried by some physiologically impossible muscular trick to open the lips by themselves, to offer an open hole to the prick I was getting desperate for. At the same time, my mounting frenzy was working itself out elsewhere, and I began to literally gobble the cock in my mouth, sucking it into my throat, lapping it, teething it gently. My hands were flying over the cocks I had curled my fingers around, jerking them frantically. And my tits were aching as

Play Time

two women sucked and licked them into their mouths. Now two fingers were in my asshole and I was clenching my cheeks to draw them in deeper.

'Fuck me,' I moaned, my lips stretched around the bulging base of Jim's hot cock.

'Fuck her,' said Melanie, 'give it to her. Shove that big black cock up that pink twat.'

'Yeaah,' Larry said in a low growl, 'yeaah.'

And he brought the tip of his cock close against the edges of my cunt lips. I moaned when I felt it and fucked my pussy harder into the air, trying to surround the silky crown.

'She's really hot,' Tom said.

'Fuck her,' said Jim.

'Fuck her, fuck her, fuck her,' they all chanted.

'Fuck me, fuck me, fuck me.' I groaned, my mouth stuffed with throbbing cock.

And with that Larry let himself drop forward and sank slowly and ponderously onto my body, his cock slicing into my cunt smoothly and surely. He entered for what seemed like an eternity, going deeper and deeper until he was hitting the farthest niche of my clutching vault. My cunt engulfed him like a sword-swallower gulps down a shaft of steel. His entry completed the circuit. I was totally plugged in. And with that, I cut loose and let myself go bananas, writhing on the rug in that strange room with nine people clustered round my body like priests around an altar, carrying out some occult rite, a sacrifice to a merciless god.

Now that other, more ancient language seized our beings and we suffered a grand glossolalia of our bodies, fucking with the same abandon which grips those who speak in tongues. The only sounds were the rasping of labored breath and the moans of ecstatic release and the quick chirping cries of climax. Jim spilled his seed in my mouth and I sucked his pulsing cock dry of cum, pulling on it with my lips until he had to force my head backwards to ease his tender prick out of my voracious grasp. He was immediately replaced by Tom, whose prong was ready to burst from the hand job I had been giving him, and I didn't miss a beat as one cock slid out and another slid in, the second easing in on the slippery coat of sperm that covered my tongue.

He must have been hotter than I thought for no sooner did his cock touch the back of my throat than he came inside me, spraying my mouth with his acrid juice. Almost like a wine taster, I could distinguish between the different flavors of sperm in my mouth as I swallowed the thick gobs of hot spunk lustily.

'What a fantastic mouth,' Tom whispered as he pumped the last of his load down my throat.

'Let me have her,' said Harvey, and as Tom slid his softening cock out from between my lips, Harvey thrust his stiff wide staff into the vacated space. Three cocks in a row spreading my lips, three cocks in a row fucking my throat, three cocks in a row being licked by my tongue! Both my hands were now free and I brought them up to the base of Harvey's cock and started jerking him off, bringing him to a climax as the head of his cock romped inside my hot cum-smeared mouth. The overall excitement of the group was so high that he was also at the edge of orgasm, and after a very brief flurry of strokes I felt the thick column begin to pulse and throb, and I opened my mouth wide to pull him all the way inside. I released my grip on the base of his cock and immediately he let loose, his pelvis twitching and the head of his prick exploding, shooting jet after jet of swirling jism on my tongue. I licked his cock lasciviously, and swallowed his cum greedily.

All this while, Larry was pumping steadily into my pussy. It was not that I had been unaware of him, but that the irresistible sensation of having three men, one after the other, cum in my mouth took priority over everything else. But now as I lay there, my lips raw and my throat rank with the taste and smell of so much sperm, two women still sucking my nipples, Larry started to move in earnest. He was propped up on his palms, his elbows locked, his huge shoulders twice as wide as mine looming over me.

'Now I'm gonna ride you, baby,' he said, 'gonna make believe you're a wall of defensive linemen and I have to screw my way through you.'

I looked up into his eyes and saw nothing but a raging fire. I couldn't know for certain whether he was in his right mind or not. But when he started moving, it really didn't make any difference. His hips combined the erratic dips of a butterfly with the brute force of a rhinoceros. The sockets must have been hinged with ball-bearings, for it didn't seem that bone and sinew could produce such fluidity and range of expression. And the power was beyond all my expectations. Although not as tall or as heavy as Jeff, he had the fullback's gift of drive, that almost inhuman thrust which is necessary to break through a wall of three-hundred-pound tacklers.

He rode endlessly, and after a while the others simply sat by the side and watched. The three men who had been sated weren't yet ready for another round, and Frank said he would fuck me next, 'after the kid had loosened her up a bit,' I hoped he had been joking, because I couldn't imagine anything heavier than what was happening. My legs were stretched to their limit, my feet high in the air. My arms went out to either side of me and my fingers curled in the thick rug. And Larry rode me with an unprecedented ferocity. His body flamed and fell and scooped and banged and raged. I could no longer feel anything but a roaring heat in my hole, a fire he kept stoking as he fucked me. After a certain point I realized that his capacity was greater than anything I had seen, and I started to let myself encompass the scope of his assault. I knew that if I allowed myself to reach for an orgasm in the same scale as the fuck he was proposing, I would blow out all my fuses. And in front of an audience to boot.

'What the hell?' I thought, and surrendered to the level of intensity Larry wanted me to experience.

Now the heat and tension really built, for each time he stroked into me, I quantum-leapt that much closer to orgasm. It was no longer simply a furrowing process whereby my pleasure came from having my pussy reamed out; it had become a cooperative venture, in which I had to match his extraordinary power with my own capacity for opening and grasping, letting him explode into the deepest recesses of my cunt and then using my cunt to clasp him tightly as he escaped. In this way I was raised to a height of striving I had never considered before, and when I was pumping and wriggling and fucking with more abandon and lustiness and simple muscular exertion that I ever had, I felt the first surge of climax building inside me.

In the same way that a body-surfer will wait out the smaller waves and put himself in position only when a truly superior wave is seen, and is then awed and somewhat frightened because the wave that is now rushing in is far more powerful that he had imagined it would be in relation to what had gone before, so I felt that the orgasm which roared through my body would turn me head over heels and plunge me into the foam until I sputtered and swallowed and perhaps drowned, my body being pulled by the underflow to a salty grave.

I don't remember precisely what happened. Arms flailing, legs kicking, piercing scream, blood pounding, heart stopping, anus opening, tits flopping, fingers curling, cunt exposing. All of that and more. My mind an irresistible steam of colors and sounds, hallucinatory shapes and intimations of endless spaces. Pure ideas shimmering like crystals in sunlight. The entire history of life on earth recapitulated in an instant. Utter clarity of understanding, sharp and dancing perceptions. A sense of bliss, of eternal happiness, of kindness and joy. Christmas bells. The entire vast and mysterious universe spinning in the center of my forehead.

And then a gradual re-adjustment, a focusing back on the ordinary reality, the mundane level of awareness. Back on the planet, in the year, in the city, in the room, in my body, and feeling Larry's cock slither out of me like a snake darting from under a slimy rock.

'Oh,' I said, encompassing everything. It was a moment when I would have given anything to be with a person, anyone, who had some inkling of the profundity of my experience, who would authenticate that what I had just felt was something special, something . . . real.

But when I looked around all I could see were hideous grins. I'm sure that they were all good people and all meant well, but they were so distant, so strange, so removed from my intimate self, that when they smiled all I could see were baboon death masks.

'Wow,' Laura Williams said, 'she really is the hottest little piece of ass I have ever seen.' She turned to her husband. 'Come on, Frank, you fuck her. Put a load up her snatch. I want to suck her pussy so bad I can hardly hold myself back. But I want to eat your cum.'

'Why don't you eat this while you're waiting,' said Tom December. His cock had become hard again, and he was staring at Laura's mouth with a salacious glint in his eyes. He held his cock in one hand. 'Come on, Laura,' he urged, 'wrap your pretty lips around this while Frank fucks the slut.'

She was already on her hands and knees and she turned toward him, walking on all fours, her eyes heavily lidded, her mouth hanging open. I saw her ass sway as she moved away from me. Harvey had begun to screw Karen in the ass, and the others were beginning to arrange themselves in new positions and combinations. I knew I was in for an all-nighter.

Frank Williams lowered his bulk over me, and curling one arm under my belly, flipped me over. 'Lift your pretty little ass in the air,' he said, 'I want to fuck you from behind.'

I didn't think there was anything left inside me, but the minute he slid his cock into my dripping pussy, I knew that I had to regain my orgasmic balance. I had flown very high, and now I was going to get very low. I put my head on the floor and began to grunt like a sow as he plowed into my insatiable hole.

Eight

The season began to gather momentum, taking on a life of its own, with a logic and direction which obliterated all other rhythms. The state of the world, wars in distant lands, poverty and restlessness in the nation, the promptings of my heart, all fell into dark shadows as the fierce light of victory blazed more brightly in our eyes. The team had not lost a game, and our collective mood was that of an army within sight of the citadel we were marching to capture. Winning the league championship, and the superbowl, meant fantastic bonuses for the players, and up to five thousand dollars more apiece for each of the cheerleaders. In addition, the prestige meant bigger crowds, and higher fees for television coverage, so that the entire operation would be bathed in an overflow of opulence. In addition, of course, there was the simple animal excitement of coming out on top. And for several weeks I forgot everything else except the great drumming excitement that filled all our days.

As so often happens when one is totally involved, I became wound up with an extraordinary tension. I wasn't aware of it until one afternoon, in the Chicago dressing room, for no apparent reason I began to tremble and weep. Sandy came over to comfort me and asked what was wrong. To my surprise, I spilled out a tale of confusion and unhappiness, feelings I had not even been aware of. I told her of what Tony had said, and how used I felt after the party at the Williams' apartment. And confessed that along with a sense of ebullience I was being slowly filled with a deep disgust of myself.

'I'm all right as long as I remember that this is all a process I'm exploring and don't identify with it,' I said at last when my sobs had subsided. 'But what with all the pressure from the season and the sex scenes I keep getting into, I can't help but crack sometimes I guess.' I smiled weakly and added, 'I'll be all right.'

She patted my cheek and said, in that delightfully brisk way of hers, 'Sugar, all you need is a little vacation to get you out of this rut. God, it's a wonder we don't all come down with the heebie-jeebies. But most of us have been around a few seasons, so I guess we're used to it. And I'm afraid that this is nothing. If the team keeps winning, by the time we reach the end of the season the tension will be enough to stun you.'

I don't know whether it was the unaccustomed tenderness, or the fact that Sandy really seemed to understand my vibrations, or perhaps a deep and long-standing desire on my part, but when I put my head against her chest to bask in her warmth, the initial feeling of friendliness gave way to a warmth which I was all too familiar with. Something stirred in my cunt, and my lips went slack, not just with relaxation but with the first stirring of desire.

I suppose she felt it too, and now that I look back on it I'm certain that she had been patiently waiting for me to arrive at that spot. What made the moment so lovely was my awareness that if I had never reciprocated, she would not have thought any the less of me or treated me more coldly. Her desire for me was clean, offered in a genuinely passive way, for me to respond to or not. And all of this without an overt gesture on her part since that first day when I walked into the dressing room and was almost swept into that vortex of female sensuality.

Sandy held my head in her hands and lifted my face toward hers. Her eyes were shining and filled with such a limpid amiability that I all but melted on the spot.

'Listen,' she said, 'we play back in Seattle next week. We can fly to San Francisco and spend five days there before the game.' She paused, kissed my lips lightly, and added, 'just the two of us. We'll get a real fancy hotel room and eat champagne and strawberries for breakfast and paint the town red. And . . . not let a man anywhere near us.' She looked deeply into my gaze. 'OK?' she said.

'OK,' I breathed. I knew that she was inviting me to have a brief fling with her, and that we would sleep together and make love and go to movies and in general behave like lovers. And at that instant, I could conceive of no more lovely thing in the world to do. I got very excited, almost like a teen-age girl, and hugged her tightly. 'Oh, Sandy,' I exclaimed, 'just to do nothing but enjoy ourselves and have fun. What a treat!'

'And no pressure, and no talk of football, or of dark brooding trainers with saturnine restrictions in their words.'

I laughed at her description of Tony, and impulsively I kissed her, just joyfully at first, but as our lips blended into one another, my mouth parted and her quick pink tongue touched my own, sending strange lava-flows of desire down into my belly. I had had peripheral sexual contact with women, the most radical being Laura Williams' ravenous sucking of my cunt after her husband blasted his sperm into me, but I had never been directly involved; it had always come about as a result of our mutual contact in relation to a man or group of men. This confrontation with Sandy challenged something in me, and while my body squirmed, my mind experienced its own form of cerebral lust, a raunchy curiosity to understand myself in this new context.

Sandy broke contact just as my hands were going toward her breasts. 'Not here,' she said. 'Let's wait until we can spread out and take our time. I dig you an awful lot and I want our first time to be right.'

In response I smiled my gratitude, and we disengaged and set immediately to packing our bags. The rest of the team was catching a flight directly to Seattle, and as we were ready to leave, Marian and Irene waltzed in, having joined the locker-room celebration after the game.

'Boy, that's fast,' Marian said.

'We're splitting for San Francisco,' Sandy told her. 'We need a vacation.'

'Oh, what a great idea,' Irene chirruped. 'Maybe I'll come too.'

'Sorry,' Sandy said, 'private party.'

The two other women exchanged arched glances. 'Well, pardon me,' Irene intoned in her best imitation of a catty voice.

The four of us looked around at one another and all burst into smiles. In a second we were all hugging in the middle of the room. Marian turned then to embrace me, 'I'm very happy about this,' she said. 'I think it will really help you to get your head straight.'

Play Time

'Not to mention her quim,' Irene purred.

She was so obviously good-intentioned that I had to hug her, despite the seeming sharpness of her words. We exchanged kisses all around, and before I could fully digest the implications of what was happening, Sandy and I were in a cab to the airport, and then in a plane heading toward that jeweled and exotic city, the place where the cataclysmic hippie movement was born. As we winged west through the sky, Sandy's hand slipped between us and her fingers intertwined with mine. I inclined my head toward her and we smiled at one another as we slipped into a light and relaxing sleep.

When we landed it was eleven o'clock, and the night was delightfully warm. We got into a taxi and Sandy surprised me by suggesting we go to North Beach before finding a hotel. 'I'd like a drink,' she said. But when we arrived on the garishly lit main drag of Broadway, she steered me into one of the topless-bottomless bars. 'It's owned by a friend of mine,' she explained.

Inside, we were among the only women in the crowd, while the stage held three naked lovelies doing their bumps and grinds. A burly affable man made his way toward us and embraced Sandy. He turned out to be the owner, and announced that drinks were on the house.

We sat and watched the show for a while, consuming three vodka martinis apiece, and the alcohol and ambience combined to make me more than a little itchy. My thighs felt as though tiny ants were nibbling at the soft flesh. The women were all slim and very sexy, and as I watched their bobbing tits and gyrating pussies, I kept reminding myself that I would soon have my mouth buried in Sandy's cunt, while her fingers explored my own. I guessed that this very reaction of mine was one of the reasons she had taken me there. As the show progressed, she began to stroke my thighs under the table, and I responded in kind, loving the feel of her firm legs beneath her short skirt.

Then, for the second time that night she surprised me. 'Like to dance?' she asked.

'Huh?' I said thickly, slightly drunk and a little turgid with swollen lust.

'Mac usually lets me get on stage and do a number. Usually I do it just for kicks and to see if there's anybody interesting in the crowd, but tonight it'll be for you. But I'd love it if you joined me.'

'Why not?' I said, looking out over the sea of piercing male eyes, imagining what it would be like to have them focused on me. I had become used to the nature of exhibitionism, and was ready to take it to its next logical step. Sandy made a gesture to the owner and when the act finished, he bounded up on stage and made his announcement in a loud voice.

'A real treat tonight,' he boomed. 'Two cheerleaders from the Seattle team, and one a dear old friend of mine' – he winked lewdly to approving chuckles – 'will grace us with a special performance. Come on girls.' And with that the small combo struck up a Latin beat.

Sandy took my hand and we made our way to the stage, all stares on us. I clambered up, almost stumbling, and suddenly found myself practically blind, powerful spotlights beaming down on me.

'Take it off,' a raucous voice shouted.

The music increased its tempo, and with a glance at one another, Sandy and I started peeling off our clothes. The crowd started stamping and whistling,

Play Time

and in a few seconds I was stark naked on the stage of a nightclub in San Francisco, a room of howling men at my feet. For a second I was paralyzed, and then the music penetrated my consciousness. Forgetting everything else, I threw myself into the rhythm of the dance, breaking into a kind of mambo shuffle. Keeping time preoccupied me for a while, but once I had the feel of the movement, I let myself go and just enjoyed the freedom of swimming through air, supported by the beating drum and thrumming guitar. I glanced over at Sandy and my heart leapt into my mouth. She was beautiful! Tits already covered with sweat jiggling back and forth, her ass trembling with each step, and the furry mound over her vulva bristling as she lifted and dropped her legs. It took a moment for me to realize that I must look exactly the same, and suddenly the stunning power of the scene hit me. I was shaking my ass to a crowd of men who were probably already erect, and only the thinnest fabric of social convention kept them from stampeding onto the stage and fucking us on the boards. With the knowledge that I was safe, I began to enjoy my cock-teasing dance. I lifted my breasts with my hands and offered them to the audience. I ran one hand between my thighs and rubbed my pussy. I turned around and shuffled from right to left, letting my cheeks wobble and shake.

The roaring of the crowd increased and men started pounding on the tables. The music hit a faster beat and a small frenzy developed. Suddenly we were out of time and space. This might have been the Coliseum in ancient Rome or an Aztec sacrificial altar. It was what it was and everything else besides. I spun around and found myself facing Sandy. We grinned at one another and started dancing to each other's movements, advancing and retreating, coming close and touching nipples, and then backing away while our hips pumped forward. It was the sublimation of sex and the prelude to sex. The vodka stirred my blood and the raw lust of the crowd raped my brain and my body leapt free of restrictions and launched into a wild orgiastic explosion, as I leapt and threw my arms about and stomped on the stage and emitted fierce cries. It was an extraordinary purgative and I wondered whether Sandy had planned this also. I took everything that had been troubling me, all my fears and self-doubts and burned them in the acid of Corybantic ecstasy, reviving the archetypal power of archaic priestesses who celebrated secret rites to gods unknown to men.

This was the antipode of the literary lesbianism which had come to form my stereotyped understanding of woman's celebration of herself. It was the spirit of the huntress in the hills, and my vision filled with eruptions of blood as I hurled myself into the climax of the dance. The audience, the music, Sandy, my life, all the sex, the doubts, all burned and dissolved in the final whirling conclusion as I spun around and around, arms flailing, tits flying, cunt gaping, until the world exploded in a single triumphant chord, and I lay on my back, panting, staring up at the twinkling stage lights, the adulating roar of the audience cascading over my ears.

I suppose that if I had been alone I would have gone on, as everyone was urging me to do, and caused such a vortex of seething passion that the whole place would have been drawn into my orbit. There would have undoubtedly been a gangbang, with the men taking me and all the other dancers in the place, and I would have easily made the front page of the *Chronicle* the next day. But Sandy helped me to my feet, gathered up our clothes, and spirited me into the dressing room.

I flung myself onto a couch and closed my eyes until everything stopped spinning. When I looked up, Sandy was watching me with undisguised desire. One of the other dancers was standing in the corner, putting on eye shadow. 'That was real pretty, honey,' she lisped, 'but it's not an easy act to follow.'

'Let's split,' Sandy whispered.

I nodded, and we dressed, and within minutes we were in our third taxi of the day. It was one of those nights when the world seems unhinged, to have lost its mundane regularity, and is no longer bothered with revolving around the sun or spinning on its axis, but has burst loose into outer space. It seemed that all convention, all law had been suspended. I was flushed with an extravagant euphoria, and felt lifted high above all humanity. I looked back on the Julie that had been weeping over her troubles just that afternoon, and from my Olympian height was able to pity her and dispense largesse. I had been catapulted into a different state of consciousness, and while I was the same person I had always been, I now, temporarily, had access to a wider range of energies.

'I feel so high,' I said to Sandy.

'That's what a vacation is for,' she replied. 'For five days you have no name, no history, no attachments. Everything is flow, everything is climax. It's time to blow out all the gaskets and let your system wax out to its fullest. So when you return to the other world, you are invigorated and refreshed.'

'Oh, Sandy,' I said, 'I'm so randy for you.'

'Me too,' she whispered. 'Soon now.'

Play Time

We took a room in one of the smaller hotels on Nob Hill, barely able to contain ourselves to go through the ritual of signing in. I let her handle all the details, and after what seemed an eternity we were in the elevator, and finally in the room, the busboy having dropped our bags and handed us the key. Sandy and I looked at one another. She was ravishing, and my desire for her was unabashed and total. As she suggested, I didn't even try to relate the moment to any other context in my life, but wanted only to experience it fully, to drain it of its juices.

Sandy glanced at me and her eyes glittered with cold intelligence. 'For five days we love each other, nothing held back. And after five days, we become friends again. All right?'

I sobered long enough to accept the full meaning of her words. I knew exactly what she was saying, and was happy that she was taking the onus of defining our relationship upon herself.

'Yes,' I breathed. 'And now, now, I want your mouth,' I said, the words spilling out of me as I ran across the room to her. I flung myself into her arms and our lips melted into a single opening while out tongues sent slithering thrills through mingled saliva.

For a long long time I was lost in the discovery of the beauty of a woman's body. Of course, I knew that women, including myself were beautiful, but mostly through reflection in men's eyes. But now I could taste and touch and smell that incredible loveliness for myself. Sandy and I shrugged off our clothing as we kissed, our hands flying from clasps to zippers to stretches of exposed flesh. We embraced and caressed, danced and stumbled, an unceasing torrent of lustful vibrations buoying us along until we found ourselves naked, sprawled across the double bed.

I didn't know what to do first. My mouth was on fire with the long complex kiss we held, my hands filled with Sandy's fullness, holding one firm conical breast, pressing it against her chest, tweaking the nipple into erection, while running my other hand over her twisting buttocks, stroking her high curved ass, running my fingers into the spreading crack. Our cunts were pressed against each other, and we pumped our hips furiously, straining for contact, my clit pounding against her pubic bone, my cunt lips tickled by her hair.

We rolled over and over, legs thrashing, tits squashed into one another's breasts, our mouths seeking voraciously to devour the entirety of the other. There was a sudden shift in rhythm, and without a word we began to revolve around one another's bellies, like two hands on a clock, our tongues parting unwillingly but continuing their agitated licking, now over shoulders, arm, tits, thighs, and finally, to the desired target.

With a groan I flung my face into Sandy's crotch, drinking in the deep smell of her juicy cunt, feeling her hair scratch my cheek. Her legs parted and her pussy lay revealed, black-rimmed and wrinkled outer lips, opening to coral curves within, and ending in a deep pink serrated bud: the hole of her hole. I curved my fingers around the edges of her twat, and stared in fascination as it parted. I was almost dizzy from the rich pungent aroma of cunt, and my mouth watered in anticipation of the feast it was about to enjoy.

I had not realized how alluring and mysterious a cunt was until then. Beneath it, the lower curves of her asscheeks provided the frame, while the insides of her long muscled thighs gave support, like two pillars holding up a temple. Above, her sloping belly. And in the center, beneath a mat of blonde curls, the soft gash itself.

'Unngh,' I moaned, and brought my lips to the core of her cunt, pressing my mouth against the already moist pussy. My jaws trembling with weakness, I curled out my tongue, and almost swooned as the acrid juices covered it. I tasted, and decided that it was the single most fantastic thing ever to hit my taste buds, at once rich and subtle.

I could control myself no longer. I lunged into Sandy's cleft, sucking and licking and nibbling. I was buried in cunt and wanted to stay there forever, drinking from that eternal fountain. I remember all the men who had gone wild between my legs, and at those times I was so taken with my own pleasure that it did not occur to me what theirs might be. Now, in retrospect, I received the vicarious pleasure from all the times I had been eaten, thinking what a wonderful thing it must be for someone to slurp-worship my twat.

The thought was obviously spurred by what Sandy was doing at precisely that moment. As I burrowed deeper between her thighs, fucking my tongue as deeply as I could into her juicy hole, pressing my lips tightly against its lips and sucking all its juices from its folds, she was doing exactly the same with me. I was so involved in the feelings coursing through my mouth that I did not at first notice the sensations in my cunt.

But now they started to reach me. Sandy had taken my clit between her teeth and was grinding it gently. This brought me so close to the edge between pleasure and pain that I shook with tension. My thighs were clamped tightly about her head, and my ass quaked as orgasmic tremors shot through me. The jolts of electricity went up my spine and into my brain and out my tongue!

The esoteric meaning of the sixty-nine position dawned on me: this was the snake swallowing its own tail, the current of cosmic unity. It wasn't me doing her or her doing me, but a single unified action in which there was no distinction between individuals. It wasn't to be my orgasm or her orgasm, but a single spasm in which we both felt the same surging conclusion. This meant there could be no manipulation, no trepidation. We would both have to surrender to the flow, and let it decide when and where we surfaced.

I let all my thoughts go and become one with Sandy's body, my mouth glued to her cunt, giving it intimate messages with lips and tongue, breathing into it, kissing it, speaking to it, while my cunt opened to her mouth, sucking in her tongue, tingling to her teeth, spending juices for her throat. My breasts were crushed against her thighs and hers against mine, while my hands fluttered again and again over the marvel of her perfectly shaped ass. I parted the cheeks and traced one finger down the crack to the small anal opening. It was already slick from the secretions and saliva that had trickled down between her thighs. The whole space from cunt to asshole was a swamp of woman-smells, a pool of thick sticky fluid.

My finger went in easily, and her tight asshole clutched it firmly. I pushed harder and soon was buried up to the third knuckle of my middle finger, and was wiggling it around, and thrusting it in and out, teasing her asshole as I lapped her pussy with broad strokes. Her finger went into my ass, and her hands pushed my cheeks inward, crushing me to her face.

Locked like that, we began to ride. With mounting pelvic thrusts and raunchy slurping sounds, we ate one another's pussies like thirsty women drinking water. I got lost in the welter of sound and motion and growing excitement. We were both cumming, that was clear, and there was no doubt but that we would cum together. Our long friendship, the shimmering night, and our impassioned fervor in the hotel room had worked us to a pitch of complete-complementarity.

Our legs kicking and sliding across the sheets, our tits rubbed sore against one another's thighs, our fingers in each other's assholes, our cunts and mouths in utter communion, we skipped like a rock skimming across the water into a series of light staggering orgasms, exploding . . . sailing . . . exploding . . . sailing . . . exploding . . . sailing . . . eight, nine, ten, eleven times, until we finally subsided, and like a stone sinking in a pond, leaving a trail of overlapping concentric circles at each place we had touched, and deep ripples where we ultimately sank.

We lay a long time without moving, side by side, our mouths still fastened to one another's pussies, our hands still inside each other's assholes. I had become a total blank, a simple movement of breath, without sensation, without thought.

'This,' I thought, 'is peace.'

And right upon my thinking it, Sandy stirred. She disengaged herself gently and rolled to the edge of the bed. She reached down to the floor, and I heard the clasps of her suitcase snap open. I didn't know what she was looking for, but her ass was so inviting I couldn't resist the temptation to do what I did next. Snaking over, I placed my mouth on the back of one of her thighs, biting firmly. Sandy gasped. I licked the bruised spot and worked my way higher, trailing inwards toward the black center where her thighs met. I glanced up and her buttocks loomed like vast hills. She spread her legs slightly and I could see between her thighs: the puckered anus, with the skin around it purple from arousal, and beneath that the gaping cunt, its crown of hair wet and straggly from pussy juices and my own saliva.

I licked the bottom of one of her succulent globes, and then dove over her rump and into the crack, my cheeks inside the spread of her cheeks. I slid out my tongue and touched her asshole lightly, causing her to squirm. I pushed forward, now bringing my lips against the tiny hole, kissing it passionately, loving its shape and taste and smell. She arched her hips and pushed back, grinding her ass into my face. I returned the pressure, hurting my mouth against the bottom of her ass crack. My tongue probed further and penetrated the arcane orifice, swirling into the hot musky canal. Sandy groaned and brought her hands back to part her cheeks further, giving me greater access to the bud at the center. I shot my tongue in as far as it would go, straining it at the root, and then pulled back, and pushed in again, fucking her asshole with my tongue. I twirled it again and drew all the way out, and then began licking the crack with broad long strokes, starting at her pussy and covering her asshole. I licked her like a dog until she was moaning steadily and audibly, and then I turned on my back and slid under her, pulling her on top of me so that she sat on my face.

Now she threw her full weight into me, and I lay back passively, my mouth open, my tongue extended, as she rubbed her bottom all over me, covering me with her cunt and asshole, grinding my head into the bed with her lust-induced rhythms. She worked more and more frantically until she was lost in another climb toward climax. I brought my hands between my legs and thrust four fingers into my cunt, plunging them in and out, sloshing into the wet center and rubbing my clit frantically. Sandy grabbed my hair and held my head in a fixed position as she rode my face, fucking my mouth with her cunt, and suddenly her motion became spasmodic and I knew that the Greater Force had overtaken her, and her gasps of climax filled my ears as her pussy juice filled my mouth, and within seconds afterwards I was kicking my legs in the air as I fingered myself into my own orgasm.

Nine

The week I spent with Sandy had a double effect. On the one hand it opened me even further erotically, for she brought me so far out and then peeled me so thoroughly, that when we returned to Seattle I was little more than a naked vibrating cunt. Any man or woman with eyes to see could have had me for the asking. But the experience also strengthened my growing dissatisfaction with impersonality in my sexual encounters. It's true that when our fling ended Sandy reverted to simple friendship, but during our days and nights in San Francisco, I wasn't just a body to her. I was the unique thing called Julie Ann DeWitt. And as we returned for the next game, I resolved that I would try to effect some kind of rapprochement with Tony, the man who had so roundly condemned me for my promiscuity.

That did come about, but not as I imagined, and only later, after the terrible party when the team won the final game of the season and assured itself of participation in the superbowl. I made it my business to run into Tony one afternoon and after some awkwardness we went out for coffee together. His manner was very reserved, even though I could read the flicker of desire in his eyes.

'Don't you fuck at all?' I asked him as we talked.

'I haven't for about eight months now,' he said. 'In fact, you're the first woman who has even vaguely interested me.'

'But why?' I asked. 'I mean, why such a long time, and why me?'

'I told you,' he explained. 'A thing is made precious by its rarity. If I were to fuck every woman who was ready to open her gap for me, my cock would fall off in no time at all. I don't want to be the anonymous stuffer, the hunk of meat that gets used to compensate for a woman's lack of inner identity. And why you? I frankly don't know. If I try to analyze it, it's hopeless. All I know is that my instincts point me toward you.'

'Well, why don't we do it?' I said.

'Because you haven't finished your trip yet. You've understood how empty all that dumb frenzied fucking is, but you have one level of hunger that still hasn't been satisfied. And until it is, you'll be edgy with any man you make it with. When I get my cock into that sweet slit of yours, I don't want to run into any barriers. I won't abide any emotional cheating, or intellectual shallowness. If I am to have you, I want the totality of you. What's the point in possessing a woman if one only gets part of the goods.'

'Aren't you embarrassed to be talking about possession?' I probed.

'You mean because of the so-called liberation of women?' He laughed. I wanted to reach out and hold his hand. His smile pierced my heart. His eyes looked into my soul. I barely knew him. Yet he seemed to have penetrated my very depths. I wanted desperately to love him. But he kept his distance. 'A woman is, of course, free,' he went on. 'And when she gives herself, that is a free choice. But having made that choice, she is then possessed by the man. He literally invades her body. Her burrows into her belly. He plants his seed in her deepest channel. After they disengage, naturally, he no longer possesses her. They regain autonomy. And she is free to make her next choice. To accept him inside her again, or not. Or perhaps to take another man. Or a woman. And the man has his yes and his no. And while my body says yes to you, Julie, my mouth says no. I don't want you now because you aren't really free. You are still obsessed. And when that final demon has left you, I will take you in my arms.'

'And then?' I asked.

'That's as far as we can know at this moment,' he continued. 'The chemistry that flows between us shall determine the shapes we assume.'

I could have sat and talked with him for hours. Not only because it was the first real conversation I'd had with a man in years, but simply to be sharing his vibration, drinking in his face, soaring on the sound of his voice.

But he stood up abruptly. 'Well, I must leave now. I'm glad we got this chance to talk,' he said.

'But can't we . . .' I began to protest.

He fixed me with a stern stare. 'I think I've made myself very clear, haven't I?'

I nodded in acquiescence and he turned quickly and walked out of the cafeteria. Subsequently I tried to remain celibate, but that made me too nervous. Tony was right; he had seen what I had known since the beginning: that I was working out some karmic cycle and could not rest until I had seen the end of it. I was afraid that if I fucked anyone else again, Tony would be turned off, but then I realized that he already knew in detail everything I had been doing all year, so nothing I did now could shock him.

So it was that with a sense of randy resignation I re-entered my pattern of activities. Practice one day a week, a game on Sundays, and the rest of the time give over to one or another form of erotic gameplay. It went that way until the end of the season, when the sun went off signalling that Seattle had won the game and the division championship, that hell broke loose.

The terrific tension that had been building all year, the balance between surging toward final victory and staying calm enough to play each game as it came, finally burst after the gun that signalled the end of the season. The fans swarmed out of the stands and roamed over the field, shouting, screaming, lifting players onto their shoulders. Three men rushed at me, picked me up bodily, and threw me into the air. They were good-natured enough, but when I landed in their arms, more than one hand grabbed my ass and squeezed my tits. But such was the exuberance of the moment that I didn't mind, and in fact squirmed around a bit and let them enjoy their lusty feels. For more than an hour the stadium was a sea of sound and movement. The other cheerleaders and I finally managed to escape into the dugout, running the gauntlet through lines of men whose lust for victory had mingled with desire for our bodies.

If I had thought the dugout would be a refuge, I was soon disillusioned. The place was packed with players, drinking champagne and emptying bottles of the foaming brew over one another's heads. Reporters shouted questions and television cameras wormed their way through the wall of tightly packed flesh. I bumped into Jeff, and for the first time since

Play Time

our horrible breakup we smiled at one another, the team's triumph dissolving all residual tension. He caught me in his arms and crushed me to him, my tits pinched by the equipment he still wore under his jersey. His hands cupped my ass and his mouth covered mine. I returned his kiss heartily and pushed my pelvis into his crotch.

He finally released me and whispered, 'See you later,' before I was swept away, spun off by the tumultuous activity all around me. A hand caught my arm and I found myself looking up into the face of Roger Edwards, who had not said a word to me since our second, aborted, date.

'How does it feel, Julie?' he shouted above the roar. 'The sweet smell of success, eh?'

I was becoming so euphoric that I even had a kiss to spare for Roger, and as my mouth went on his, his tongue darted between my lips. At the same time he squeezed one of my tits, and then moved away quickly, leaving me gasping.

From time to time I caught a glimpse of Sandy and the other cheerleaders weaving in and out of the male giants who dominated the relatively small space. Some of the wives were there, including Laura and the other women I had 'swung' with. I looked for Tony but couldn't see him anywhere. Every three minutes more champagne was poured into my glass. And the room soon became a dizzy whirl of overheated vibrations and flashing glances.

The mood was definitely orgiastic, although it never occurred to me that there could be any actual sexual activity in that space. When I thought about it at all, I imagined that I would wind up with a bunch of the men and a couple of women at someone's apartment, fucking until dawn. But more time passed than I knew, and without my being aware of it, the camera crew slipped out, along with reporters, and everyone else who did not belong in one way or another to the team. How it occurred I will never understand, but a moment arrived in which I was the only woman left in the locker room. I had been drinking and flirting and kissing and dancing about, lost in the general uproar, and I guess Sandy and the other cheerleaders made their own connections and were whisked away to different pads.

My first clue as to what was happening came when I glanced toward the opening of the dugout and saw that the doors had been closed. The radio was still blasting out a succession of harsh rock songs, and many of the men were still shouting and horsing around. But the crowd had definitely thinned, and a subtle change in the ambience crept over the space. More of the players were following me with their eyes and my ebullience lost some of its edge as I realized that I stood in the center of the locker room, dressed in my tight shirt and very brief skirt, while more than forty men gradually stopped their random celebrating and began to focus on me.

They ranged from fully dressed, complete with shoulder pads and uniform, to wearing nothing but jock straps. The place smelled of booze and raw animal sweat. They were still covered with dirt from the field and they resembled nothing so much as a small army that had just spent a month in the trenches. And I appeared as the first woman they were setting their eyes on.

Nervously, I began to back toward my dressing room, but as I moved sideways I bumped into Rick Folsom, the center. I looked up at him and saw the unmistakable gleam in his eyes.

'Where you going, Julie?' he said, leering.

'Uh, just going to get dressed,' I said in a low voice.

'Got to get undressed first, don't you?' he taunted.

'Well, yes,' I mumbled, 'I was intending . . .'

But I didn't get a chance to finish the sentence. 'The least we can do is help you get undressed,' he said in a loud voice. And then pitching his voice so that it covered the whole room, he added, 'The least we can do is help Julie undress, can't we boys? In appreciation for everything she's done for us this season.'

'Please,' I said. The moment could have been overwhelmingly erotic, but as they massed and moved toward me, the only sensation I could feel was fear. There were at least forty of them, and they weren't in a gentle mood.

'Please what?' John Carrol said as he stepped toward me. He was one of the men I had fucked during the year, and he had found his special form of enjoyment in hearing me beg for his cock. I knew that he was reminding me of that.

'This can't be happening,' I thought, and tried to picture what might come to rescue me. But I knew that the stands were long since empty, and that no one would be coming through those locked doors.

Rick slipped his hand under my shirt from behind and began to hoist it above my shoulders. I tried to push it down, but two men sprang forward to help him. In an instant seven or eight of them were holding me, grabbing me by the ankles and wrists and waist. I kicked and twisted, but it was of absolutely no use. Ineluctably, they got what they wanted, and I moaned as my shirt was ripped from my body, exposing my bare tits to their eyes. Quickly, my skirt

Play Time

was unhooked and my panties yanked off, and then I was naked, my cunt visible and accessible to the entire mob of lust-crazed football players.

While I was annoyed at their presumption, I can't deny that I responded to the intense massive erotic charge that was being poured into my pussy. Their eyes seemed to smolder and their faces were distorted into masks of sensual cunning.

I decided to follow my father's advice, which was to make the best of any situation. Resistance would breed violence and faced with more than eighty times my body weight in the form of a gang of huge fierce men, I realized that my best hope lay in surrender.

So I stopped struggling and let my head fall back and relaxed my stomach. I gave them the Julie that existed in their imaginations, the slut whose label was indelibly marked across the top of her pubic hair. I didn't know if my body could take it, but I had no choice.

'That's better,' one of the men said. 'You know you want it.'

'Come on,' another voice shouted. 'Let's fuck her.'

One of the cots from the cheerleaders' dressing room was brought out and I was tossed on it. I landed with legs apart, my tits flopping wildly. Not an instant passed before they were all over me. I felt like the victim of an automobile accident lying in the street while a crowd milled around to rubberneck at my body. Only they weren't content with watching.

Hard rough hands gripped my tits, pummeling the soft flesh and pinching the tender nipples. Fingers pulled at my cunt lips and poked insolently into my ass crack. A cock thrust itself between my lips and began fucking my face rapidly. Another cock slipped into my twat and started thrusting in and out with pounding strokes. From the sheer impact of all that flesh, my cunt got wet and lubricated the stiff pole that ravaged it.

'Oh, yeah,' hissed the man fucking me. 'She's getting wet. She's getting wet. She's getting hot.'

The excitement must have been too much for him for he came almost at once, and I could feel his cum splashing inside me. Another took his place immediately. And once more my pussy yawned to take a prick inside itself. The man above me came in my mouth, forcing his cock into my throat so that it spurted down the tube and into my belly. I had to swallow to keep from choking. And again, no sooner had he finished then another took his place, sliding his thick cock on my slippery tongue.

Some were sucking my tits, biting the nipples, causing more pain than pleasure. I groaned but the sound was stiffled by the pole of meat stuffing my face. Calloused fingers dug into my ass as a third man started to fuck me, the second having already deposited his sperm in my cunt. My cheeks were pulled apart and a finger rudely thrust into the asshole.

'I want to fuck her butt,' a rough voice said. 'Hurry up and finish so I can have her ass.'

Almost more than the specific actions of the men who were fucking and feeling me, I could feel the urgency of the others, the almost two score who pushed in from behind, watching with avid looks as I was displayed, my legs held high in the air. I could feel their eyes ravishing my bruised tits, lapping at my pussy, boring into my ass, hungering after my mouth.

'Tits and ass and mouth and cunt,' I sang to myself as they humped me into oblivion.

I began to pump my pelvis back and forth, and to roll my hips around on the cot. The movement sparked something in me, and I felt the first rushes of genital pleasure as the fourth man mounted me and started his ride. They were all cumming quickly, probably due to the white-heat intensity of excitement in the room. For so many men to gang-bang a pretty young girl must have roused all their archetypal modalities of male sexuality.

After a while I lost count of numbers and lost track of time. I don't know how many entered me, or what hour it was. It occurred to me that when they finished, those who had gone first would be ready for seconds. My mouth was a pool of semen. It caked on my gums and lodged under my tongue and stuck to the roof of my mouth and splashed up my nose. Men came in my mouth and on my lips and all over my face.

A dozen times I was turned over, sometimes to be fucked from behind, but more often to have my asshole reamed. I cried out at first but by the third man my anus was as loose as my pussy, and they fucked me there with total ease. I was stood up and bent over, rolled to my side, made to kneel, and screwed from every conceivable angle.

As the thing hit full stride, I could not remain passive even if I had wanted to. So much energy, so much power, so much consistent and terrible penetration in all my openings had weakened a final wall of reserve, probably the spot Tony had mentioned. And I knew that this was the moment when I would have to break through once and for all, to irrevocably take my fill of sexual excitement so that it would no longer drive me.

Play Time

I started to move with the men fucking me, humping my cunt into the succession of cocks that entered me, sucking on the pricks that slid into my mouth and tonguing them avidly. When I was fucked in the ass, I shocked my hips back and slammed my buttocks into the thighs of whichever man was behind me, clamping my muscles tight and draining his cock dry.

In short, I let myself go wild. I became a mindless, moaning, gurgling spasm of sexual frenzy. I flailed about, shaking my ass violently, licking my tongue up to lap whatever was placed there, cock or asshole or mouth. I grabbed cocks with my hand and jerked them back and forth with total abandon, giving all the handjobs I had ever given as a teenager, forgiving myself for all the boys I had left hanging after a night of heavy petting.

The sounds that came from my throat were something that no animal could ever make; the howls of a human who had descended to a level below beasts. I didn't care any more, didn't care if I died. This was the logical conclusion of my decision to follow Jeff, and I would live to the fullest. I begged, I bleated, I crawled. And still they came, their livid cocks piercing me again and again, until I was little more than a twitching rag doll, fluttering aimlessly to each intrusion.

Time passed and I noticed a change in tempo. There weren't as many men as there had been. In the distance I heard showers running and figured that some were washing and dressing and leaving.

I was as one drugged and was only vaguely aware of them taking me outside, onto the field itself. I could feel the turf on my back and above me loomed the white goalposts. And as perhaps the thirtieth load of sperm exploded on my tongue I passed out . . .

Ten

I awoke to the sound of temple bells and Buddhist chanting. I opened my eyes and found myself lying on a very low bed in a large cheerful room. One entire wall was glass and opened onto a vista of distant mountains. It was a clear blue day and the sun seemed to be directly overhead.

'It must be about noon,' I thought.

I tried to move and found that my body was a vast complex of aches. Easing myself slowly, I slid another pillow under my head so I could half sit up. I lifted the sheet covering me and looked down on my body. Black-and-blue marks dotted the skin. My breasts especially seemed a mass of bruises, and when I brushed a finger over my nipples I shuddered with the memory of pain. I could almost see the thumb prints embedded in the pink tips.

From the next room the deep rumble of a single monotonous chant rose and fell, interspersed with the clacking of beads and the ringing of a small bell. I could smell the faint aroma of incense.

'Where the devil am I now?' I thought.

I slid my hand down and tentatively touched my pussy. It seemed intact. I slid one finger inside, and realized that it had been coated with a soothing balm. The membrane was extremely sore and tender, but the organ was resilient and firm. I realized that I had been bathed, dabbed with antiseptic ointments, and bandaged in several spots.

I took a deep breath and was surprised that despite everything else, basically I felt healthy and refreshed. I was warm and comfortable, and filled with that joyous sense of well-being that comes after a high fever has broken. I was clean, not only outside, but in my soul. I had been purged; I knew that as sharply as the reality of the strong light that poured in through the window.

I drifted off to sleep again, dozed for a few moments, and when I awoke again the sounds from the next room had stopped. I slid back a bit more to raise myself to a sitting position, deciding to wait to see what happened.

Within a few minutes, the door opened. I looked over and saw a tall thin man, dressed in a *yukata*, the informal kimono that Japanese wear around the house, walking toward me. He was carrying a tray holding two huge tumblers of freshly squeezed orange juice and two mugs of steaming coffee. The apparition was so startling that for a few seconds I didn't recognize who it was, but then his features suddenly snapped into place and I gasped with surprise.

'Tony,' I breathed, 'it's you.'

'I trust you slept well,' he said in an easy conversational tone as he knelt by the bed and placed the tray on the floor next to me.

'What are you doing here?' I exclaimed.

'Why, I live here!' he replied. And then with a playful smile, added, 'And what, may I ask, are *you* doing here?'

'I don't know,' I said, my eyes wide with wonder.

'Well, I do,' he answered, 'and as soon as you

drink your juice I'll tell you.'

He handed me a glass and I sipped the delicious chilled pulpy juice down, feeling its revitalizing power fill my body. I was amazed at how good I felt.

'I got an insane phone call sometime around midnight,' he said. 'It took me ten minutes to sort out the story, then I rushed over to the stadium and found you where he had left you. For a minute I was afraid you were dead, but I realized that it would take more than a forty-man gangbang to do you in.'

His tone was teasing, and I wondered how he could be so lighthearted about such a terrible occurrence. I glanced over at him, a little embarrassed that he had seen me in such a state, but his eyes were steady and warm. It seemed that nothing could ruffle this man.

He picked up his cup and sipped at his coffee, staring into space for a long time. For the first time since I was a child, I could hear the quality of silence; not merely the absence of sound, but the vibrant vitality of the creative void itself. It was as though Tony had entered a profound meditative state, although there was nothing about his posture or facial set which indicated anything but simple reflectiveness and relaxation.

'This may seem odd to you, Julie,' he said at last, 'but I want you to see something.' He went into a drawer of the low table next to the bed and pulled out a stack of photographs.

'You know, when I saw you there, it was something close to a mystical experience. You had reached the bottom of the pit of degradation and had become so grotesque that you transcended categories altogether and emerged as a creature of unearthly beauty. I took these because I knew that such a moment could never occur again.'

He handed me the pile of photos and I leafed through them slowly. They were all Polaroid snapshots, taken with a flash, and all portrayed me, from a dozen different angles and far away to extremely close up. He was right. Unconscious, twisted, dirtied, naked, I presented a picture of such complete surrender that an eerie beauty was born. I saw myself as some kind of sacrifice, the slaughtered virgin on the altar of professional football, and even the white goalpost served to augment the image, rising ghost-like and symbolic over my shattered body.

'What are these for?' I asked.

'For me to look at from time to time,' he said. 'And for nothing else or no one else. They have a meaning for me that I won't try to explain, even to you. But they provide the key I've been looking for ever since I met you, the understanding of why I am so powerfully drawn to you.'

'Tony,' I protested, 'you mean that you found me in that brutalized state and you took the time to snap all these photographs of me?'

'Well, I didn't take the pictures at once,' he replied. 'I had to go to my locker to pick up the camera.' And with that he laughed, obviously enjoying some private joke.

'What's so funny?' I said, my voice rising.

'Oh, the obviousness of things,' he replied. He took out the pack of cigarettes that was stuck in the sash around his waist, lit one, and commenced staring into space once more.

'Tony,' I said, 'what's happening?'

'I'm afraid I don't know,' he told me, blowing out a cloud of smoke. 'I'm not too much different from you. Some years ago I graduated from college, and joined the Marines. There I received an education that made me rethink everything I'd learned to date. I was stationed in Japan, and had the good fortune to meet a master of erotic arts. At the same time I was introduced to certain meditation techniques. When I got discharged, the job as trainer and coach presented itself to me. I had come to the conclusion that the healthiest – both physically and psychologically – way I could earn a living was to do something that involved the vigorous use of my body. I have no worldly ambitions as far as career is concerned; my real work is of a different nature altogether. And so I've been working for the Seattle team, and living my life, and doing a lot of travelling off-season. I'm really quite content.'

'And how do I fit in?' I asked.

'That's curious,' he said. 'I've been aware for some time now that I need a mate, someone to complement me. Also, someone to make love with. And since I realized that whoever she was would be chosen for me by the same Force to which I have surrendered the rest of my life, I have been waiting for a sign. And as I told you, when I saw you, I knew that you were probably the one.'

I shook my head in wonder and disbelief. He sounded so certain of himself, so confident, that I felt there had to be a flaw somewhere.

He must have read my thoughts for he went on, 'I don't expect you to understand all at once. In fact, I'm just learning about it myself, what it's like to live by faith. You have no idea how chagrined I was when I began to find out what you were up to. The orgies, the violent sex, the perversions. Again, I have nothing against any of that as an activity in itself, but that you were so indiscriminate had me doubting my intuition. And then I started to see that you were being prepared, you were being taken through a complete cycle of a certain kind of abandonment. That, in a word, you were being *trained*, by destiny, to exorcise all the residue of false sexuality that everyone in this society is heir to. And then I knew that I had only to wait, to have patience until you were clear, and came out the other side. And then we would be free to find one another.'

'If that's a declaration of love or a proposal of marriage,' I said, 'it's the least unromantic one I've ever heard.'

'You have no conception of true romance,' he shot back, an edge to his voice. 'You still think that romance is a feeling; you don't understand that it's a world view, a sublime discipline, a path that very, very few can follow successfully, and one laid with more traps than the mind can imagine.'

Despite the fact that he was melting my resistance with every word, a resistance not to him but to the vision he was creating before my eyes, I tried to hold my ground, even though in my heart I was fiercely certain that he was speaking my deepest, most secret fantasies.

'Well, what happens now?' I asked, attempting to rise to sarcasm, 'do I just fall into your arms or do you have a detailed blueprint which will tell me how to behave?'

He put out his cigarette, stood up, unwrapped the sash, and let his robe fall to the floor. He stood before me completely naked. And he was extraordinarily beautiful, with a body like a dancer's, slim, the muscles long and pliant instead of knotted tightly. He was covered with a very fine down, except for his chest where a thick patch of black hair erupted, and

Play Time

the triangle between his thighs, the mat of curly brown pubic hair. His cock was soft, and hung full and curved from his crotch. Even in that state it was thick and long, succulent, as though filled with juicy pulp. The crown flared out in violet grandeur, impassive and hooded. His eyes shone with a strange light, and for a moment I thought I was in the presence of a god.

'What you have seen up to now,' he said in a measured tone, 'has been merely the personality. Now you are looking at the body. And soon you will see the essence itself. And then you will know what to do.'

He walked around to the other side of the wide mattress, sat down facing me, and folded his legs. His hands pressed down on his knees, palms toward the ground. He took a deep breath, and his gaze went inward. I don't know quite how to explain what took place, but it was as though he disappeared. He was there, and yet he wasn't.

I watched him for perhaps five minutes, my heart racing. And then he returned his gaze outward and pierced into the space behind my eyes with his glance.

'I can instruct you in techniques, and I will, slowly. But more important than that is the structure of our flow. The movement must begin with you; you must have the impulse, you must initiate. And I will serve as the unmoving point around which your dance takes place. I can be no more than the focus.' He paused. 'Do you understand?'

'You mean I'm the one who gets on top,' I said.

Tony laughed, a deep, warm, reassuring sound. 'Yes,' he said, 'although the position can vary. Later, we can lie side by side, in equality. And on rare occasions we can enter the animal mode, with me providing the thrust. But the central idea, and the one which will form the basis of all our erotic activity, will involve your being the one who decides the time of our union.'

Something tugged at my brain. 'Wait a minute,' I said, 'what if I don't want to get into anything with you? What if I put on my clothes and walk out and never see you again?'

'I do not own you, I do not hold you, I do not control you. I am the self-contained. Again, I tell you, the decision to come or go, to join or pull apart, is completely yours.'

I sat up, throwing the sheet off me, disregarding the twinges of pain. A current of anger had begun to run through me. 'You've got it all figured out, haven't you?' I said. 'You've come to your conclusions and now you think you can get me to go along with your game plan.'

Tony raised one hand, palm forward. It was a gesture that meant *stop*, but I recognized it as one appearing on Burmese statues of Buddha. 'I have to keep reminding you,' he told me, 'that I desire nothing. I have revealed to you everything that I am. And now you must decide whether you are in accord with that or not. There's nothing personal in any of this.'

'That's just the trouble,' I exploded. 'It's all so fucking impersonal. You act as though I were a figure on a diagram instead of a person.'

'What you identify as a person,' he replied, 'is just our separative ego. That's as relevant to your true identity as that sign across your belly.'

His remark caught me up short, and in that moment of abrupt stillness, I realized that I had become quite aroused. It was not a specifically erotic feeling, for it had none of the sharp focus of lust. By my entire body surged with energy and my mind crackled with alertness. I found myself moving toward Tony without having had any conscious desire to do so.

'How is this different from any other trip?' I asked, slightly maddened by his imperturability. 'I mean, what you're telling me sounds very grand, but in effect it's just another offer from a man, isn't it?'

'Well, I'm a man and you're a woman, he said drily. 'I suppose that that aspect of our interaction has to enter in at some level. And, of course, you're free to view things from any angle you desire. For myself, if I'm going to assume any viewpoint at all, I prefer it to be the loftiest possible.'

He seemed unassailable and as I watched him I pondered the many aspects of the confrontation. Having behaved in a scrupulously gentlemanly manner, having spoken to me with only forceful honesty, having rescued me from the dangerous situation of the previous night, knowing all about my record of debauchery and overlooking it as lightly as he might a trivial bad habit, this man now sat naked before me and offered me a relationship in which our erotic life would be led solely by my impulses. And beyond all this, I would have absolute freedom to come or go as I pleased, whenever I wanted.

And at once I saw the subtle trap of his disclosures. For if I began to taste the heady froth of such a relationship, I would never be able to settle for anything less. And since it would be nearly impossible to find another man who operated consistently on that level, I would find myself bound to Tony.

'But this all implies marriage,' I said.

Play Time

'I'd rather call it mating,' he replied. 'The connotations of the other word are too misleading.'

'And how would we live?' I went on. 'Where? What kind of life style? Would you expect me to chant with you and become a Buddhist or whatever the hell you are?'

Before the words left his mouth, I knew what he would say. 'I expect nothing,' he told me.

Almost like a commando attempting a last-ditch effort to find a chink in an enemy's defenses, I went for his cock. I had climbed to such a pitch of generalized excitement that I needed to give the energy some form, and as a cloud of electrons will be polarized and release their charge in a single sizzling bolt of lightning splitting the sky and striking whatever object is unfortunate enough to rise sufficiently above the ground to attract the jagged thunderbolt, so the electricity in and around my body gathered at the base of my spine, rose up the s-curved column, and shot out of my tongue. I fell forward very slowly and my head dropped into his lap where his turgid cock met my already sucking lips.

'Now we'll see just how cool he is,' I thought as I curled my tongue under his prick and took it into my mouth.

For a few minutes I tried every cocksucking trick I knew. Licking, nibbling, sliding the shaft down to the base of my throat, biting the tip gently. I rolled around on the bed as though groveling before him, giving him full view of my ass. I rubbed my tits against the sheets, stoking the fires of my own desire. I held the base of his cock with my hands and jerked it back and forth, stuffing him inside me.

Tony got hard very slowly. His cock came to life like a sleeping man gradually waking into consciousness. It was as calm as he was, and I knew that he was allowing the pleasure I gave him to seep into his skin. There was no grabbing, no haste, no urgency on his part. All that came from me. Which, I recalled, is how he had said it ought to be.

While I tried to resent finding myself in the position I had fought against, I could not deny that I experienced a dimension of erotic enjoyment I had not known before. I felt, amidst my growing arousal, a sense of vast space, of endless time. It was as though what was happening was not just a limited act, with a beginning, middle, and end, but an ongoing process, a general movement which was proceeding eternally and of which we were merely the momentary symbols.

I lost myself in my reflections as I let my body do its ritual, and before I was conscious of its occurrence, Tony's large, beautifully sculpted cock was stiff and throbbing in my mouth.

I feasted on its length and shape, treating my tongue to the textural smoothness of the flaring crown. I buried my face in his crotch, letting the phallus slide deep into my throat. I licked its veined underbelly, and covered its taut skin with glistening saliva. Unhindered, appreciated, I lavished love upon the rigid principle of creation.

I pulled back and looked up into Tony's face. His eyes were lidded, seeing me but not staring. His gaze was as impassive as if he were watching a sunset, and filled with as much of a sense of wonder. His body was still. I ran my hands up his chest and was barely able to feel his heartbeat. There was not a whisper of urgency in the coursing of his blood.

I slid up his torso, flowing the movement of my arms. My hands went around his neck, my legs curled behind his buttocks. And with a small easy movement, I covered his cock with my moist and tingling cunt.

As he slid into me, as I lowered myself onto him, a low sigh escaped my lips. He filled me totally, perfectly. The inside of my cunt was sore, but all my stiffness and pain faded to the background. I leaned my head against his chest, my breasts pressing into his ribcage, and tightened the clasp of my legs and arms. I embraced him totally, and opened deep inside myself as he penetrated into my core.

We sat like that for a very long time, not moving, until our breaths became as gentle as those of a sleeping infant. More than any superficially sexual sensation, I felt a deep and abiding completion, a joining which held intimations of a real union. Everything else – thoughts, emotions, the structures of mundane existence – melted and ran off my soul like ice yielding to the mid-day sun. I entered a state of awareness which soared beyond all words, beyond all meaning, a gentle undifferentiated bliss which in truth had nothing to do with my much-vaunted individuality.

To speak would have been blasphemous, and so I remained silent.

Then, something stirred. I can't even give it a name or a reason. Simply, suddenly, there was movement. It manifested in my body, but was not only physical. I neither wanted nor did not want to move; the impulse was an imperative from a source far deeper than I could conceptualize. At first slowly, and then with mounting rapidity, I began my dance. My arms began a pattern in the air, a serpentine slithering through space. My shoulders rotated, and my chest swung back and forth, the right and left sides in rhythmic alternation, causing my breasts to sway.

Play Time

My hips rolled, forming figure-eights along the dorsal plane, circles along the lateral. With that, my buttocks churned across his thighs. And all of this centering finally in my cunt, which had become a turbulent sea of incredibly complex gyrations, swarming over the cock which pierced it like a hundred waves of ants sweeping over an immense log on the forest floor.

The movement found its necessary expression, and once established, began to increase in range and tempo. I started to spin into a state of transcendent awareness, losing myself like a dervish in the dance. I climbed higher and higher as the spirit of exhilaration seized me in its soaring spiral. Shivers shot through my flesh, my nipples felt like burning coals, my ass sang in an ecstasy of abandon, and my cunt grew dizzy with delight, rejoicing in its heat and wetness and scintillating sensation and, above all, in its utterly unique and totally detached intelligence. It felt itself at last as the complement and complete equal to the organ which had usurped supremacy so early in life and assumed control of the direction of my being. The cunt finally arrived at the understanding that it was its own brain.

A roaring swept through me, an effusive unfolding; my body flew into a vast consuming convulsion and I thrilled throughout every fiber with the overwhelming orgasm. The climax went on for minutes, and subsided slowly, leaving me pumping my pelvis spasmodically into Tony's cock.

Once again we became quiet, and I slid back into the silence, the unity, the state of undifferentiated awareness. I held him loosely, simply feeding him, his strength, his solidity, his unshakable centeredness. And when I had lost all sense of being separate, when there was no longer an 'I' in my consciousness, the movement began again, and again swept me through the many states of the dance, until I soared into orgasm, a climax which did not have the abrasive quality of an explosion but came rather as the rapid fluttering of wings seen just before a seagull lands upon the water.

The cycle repeated itself countless times, and although the physical manifestation was almost the same in each instance, the tone of each phrase uncovered a new modality, pointed to a different dimension, a deeper aspect. It was obvious that the process was open-ended and infinite. I don't know how long we went on. I didn't become tired, for it seemed that no energy was lost. Instead it passed back and forth between us, with each passage providing another purification of the erotic vibration, until the act was a single sustained hum.

There came a point at which I suddenly knew that we had finished. Tony said nothing, remaining still and silent as he had throughout, although I never for an instant doubted his total and intense participation. It was, again, a signal from some source I could not identify which, as it were, tapped me on the shoulder and suggested that I bring the movement to an end. I lifted my face, kissed Tony on the lips, and gently raised my body, sliding my cunt off his rigid cock.

We sat facing one another for a long time, his cock slowly sinking back into its lax downward curve, and my body's functions returning to their normal moderate speed. The veil which had surrounded us parted slowly, and mundane reality re-asserted its mood. I stretched, and realized I was ravenously hungry.

It was only then, as I regained a sense of my usual level of awareness, did I get a sense of just how far out I had been.

'Tony,' I said, 'that was . . .' I didn't have the words.

'Yes,' he said. 'I've never experienced it so totally and for such duration. But it bears out the textual descriptions with amazing accuracy.'

I was dumbfounded to hear the man with whom I had shared such an extraordinary afternoon talk as though we had been demonstrating some proposition of theoretical physics. 'Textual descriptions!' I shouted, returning to my ordinary level of emotional reality with a sharp bounce, 'were you fucking me or a book?'

'To be precise,' he said in his calm voice, 'you were doing the fucking. I merely provided the stage upon which the dance could take place. In addition, it must have occurred even to your obstinately contrary mind that what has been occurring for the past five hours does not fit into any of the categories of personality.'

'Five hours!' I said. I turned and looked out the window. It was dark outside. 'Have we been fucking for five hours?' I asked. 'No wonder I'm so hungry.' A spurt of sentimentality gushed through me and I batted my eyelashes coyly and said, 'It was wonderful, Tony.'

'Good God,' he said, uncoiling his legs and rolling off the bed. He stood up and bent over to massage his thighs and knees. He peered up at me, smiled warmly, and went on, 'Just my luck to find my Shakti and have her turn out to be a Betty Boop devotee.'

He rose to his full height, and held out his arms. I rose off the bed and went to embrace him. He held me tightly, his arms pulling me toward his hard chest.

'Ooh,' I sighed, 'I was beginning to think you didn't have any feeling at all.'

He stepped back, held me at arms' length, and let his gaze roam over my face. 'Feelings are just things we have, like noses and fingers and ideas. We can enjoy them and express them, but they can never in themselves, be the cause of anything lasting. It's not that I don't have feelings, but that I don't give them any special importance.'

'Not even love?' I asked.

'Love is the purest form of energy available to a human being. What we did on that bed was an inkling of that truth. In fact, sex is itself a meditation on love, no more, no less. Love is the supreme manifestation of the Force which sustains all the forms of creation. It is, and does not take an object. You and I can enter the field of love together, but it is misleading for me to say, "I love you". I may love, and you may love, and if we merge our fields of energy, then we love together. The love which attaches to a specific person is only a shadow, an example, of the universal love of which everything is but a symbol.'

My eyes were sparkling and my heart was full, and yet my mind resisted. 'I can agree with all that as an idea,' I said, 'but it has no meaning unless I can feel it.' I put one hand between my breasts. 'Here,' I added.

'My idea, and your feeling, and our bodies. This is the triangle which lies at the core of creation. The greatest mistake a man can make is to insist that a woman think as he does; the greatest mistake a woman can make is to insist that a man feel as she does; the greatest mistake a man and woman can make together is forget that each needs the other's body to complete the circuit of energy in which bliss is found.'

He dropped his arms and stepped back. 'Are you as hungry as I am?' he asked, abruptly changing tone.

We went into the kitchen and prepared a very late breakfast of eggs and home fries and toast and fruit. I found myself moving about the room as though I had lived in the apartment a long time.

'What do you think – excuse me, feel – about moving in with me?'

'I don't know,' I told him, pouring hot water over the coffee grinds. 'It sounds silly to say after what we've been through, but I barely know you.'

I realized that I had matured quite a bit since impetuously taking Jeff up on the same offer.

'I need to think about it,' I added, 'but in my heart I want to say yes.'

'There's no rush to decide,' he said.

We ate slowly, and in silence. At one point, one of the hundreds of questions that had been racing through my mind came to my lips and without considering, I asked, 'Did you cum, Tony?'

He laughed, the same open expression of simple pleasure, and again, it seemed to point to a joke which was utterly private to him alone.

'I didn't ejaculate, if that's what you mean.'

'But aren't you frustrated?'

'Not in the least.'

'I don't understand,' I said, for perhaps the tenth time that day.

'I'll give you a couple of books to read,' he told

me. 'It's too tedious to explain without your having some rudimentary knowledge of the concepts I'm involved with.'

I wanted to press him further, but he stood up. 'There's a program on at seven I don't want to miss,' he said.

'Television?' I asked.

'It's another form of meditation,' he said.

I suppose my face must have registered annoyance, for he added, 'Please don't have any preconceptions about me, Julie. I don't want to perform for you, nor explain overmuch. Learn about me as I am.'

'But it seems so odd. After what we shared today and all your talk of exalted states, how can you do something so . . . so *bourgeois*?'

'I'm very bourgeois,' he said. 'I had a very conventional middle-class upbringing, a standard education, and I work at a rather routine job. I'm just an average man. Enlightenment does not stand outside history, and spirituality is nothing more than accepting one's true nature, in all its sublime *and* banal manifestations. Despite the fact that I am in touch with a deeper reality, in the way I live my life I am very, very ordinary.'

'And what shall I do while you're watching the tube?' I asked, sounding peevish and not really liking myself for it.

'I don't know,' he said. 'Do the dishes, maybe, or come and watch with me, or . . . whatever you like.'

'Or maybe I'll return to my place,' I flung at him.

'Please don't threaten me,' he replied softly. 'I won't fight with you. I have no desire to dominate or be dominated. I'm bored by that kind of challenge. Of course, as I've had to remind you a number of times, you are absolutely and unconditionally free.

So you can do what you wish. But if you remain at the level of infantile intimidation, what you get in return won't be very interesting.'

'That's very high-sounding,' I said. 'But the fact remains that you want to have your cake and eat it too. You want to stay wrapped up in your world of private fantasy – excuse me, *vision* – and not have me disturb you at all, and yet you want me to climb aboard your cock and fuck you silly. Pardon my crude language, but that's the bald truth of it, isn't it? You're just like any other man. You want your piece of ass when you want it, and otherwise you don't want to be bothered.'

'You're merely reformulating, in your refreshingly saucy language, the basic contradiction which defines male and female. It is my mind and your feeling locked in tension with each other. And it is only in our bodies that that duality can be resolved. I'm no more happy with that polarity than you are; but there it is, it's one of the givens of creation, and all we can do is deal with it intelligently.'

'Which means your way,' I shot out.

'It's the way I've chosen, but it's been in existence for at least five thousand years. I really can't claim that it's *my* way. When our bodies are joined, we complete the triangle. When they aren't, we must remember not to let the inherent contradiction become antagonistic, nor pretend that it isn't there. We must know how to be neutral, to let one another *be*.'

He frowned for a moment, staring at the wall over my head, and then he added, 'We can't possibly solve all this right now. And there's no point in getting so intense we wind up tied into knots. I'm going in to watch television. You can join me, or make yourself comfortable in any way you like. And if you really want to leave, I'll drive you back.'

'Oh, I wouldn't want you to miss your program,' I snapped, wondering why I was being so nasty.

'I'm sorry that this has to happen, Julie. Believe me, I don't relish pain and negative emotions. But if this is who we are right now, then it must be borne.'

'Mr. Generosity himself,' I said, my voice dripping with scorn.

Tony came at me with total deliberation. 'I've asked you for nothing,' he said, his face a mask of controlled anger. 'I've been honest with you. And this afternoon I gave you some inclination of what real sex could be. On top of this I have offered you my apartment, and have tried to remain reasonable while you have lacerated me with anger, sarcasm, and threats. All this after I allowed myself to become vulnerable to you. You have behaved like some debased and vicious criminal. And now you demand, with an arrogant toss of your head, that I somehow entertain you, that I have no right to do what I want but must provide for your whimsical desires, as though I were a court jester and you a queen. It's not like that, Julie, and whether you have been chosen for me by destiny or not, if you can't exhibit at least a minimum of simple, decent human concern, then you can put your rags back on your shoulders and crawl back to the animals who used you and discarded you last night.'

With that he turned sharply on his heel and walked into the next room.

I sat for a long time, a swirl of mixed feelings and inchoate thoughts, my body still throbbing from our extraordinary fucking. I felt paralyzed. To leave at

Play Time

the moment would have been heartbreaking, to say painful. If I fought to maintain my integrity, Tony and I would be at one another's throats. If I submitted, I would despise myself eventually. Despite that fact that this relationship came couched in a vastly different vocabulary, offered a highly sophisticated eroticism, and promised total individual freedom for each of the partners, underneath all that the same old man-woman mechanics were at work, tapping out the same message: you can't live with the opposite gender, and you can't live without it.

I got up and walked toward the next room, uncertain of what I would do. But as I reached the doorway, Tony stepped up to the same spot, coming from the opposite direction.

'Tony,' I said, 'why is it so difficult?'

'It's not difficult,' he said, cheerfully, 'it's impossible.'

'Then what are we going to do?'

'Well, I'm going in to get a soda and then watch the rest of this program.' He kissed me on the forehead. 'I won't be your father, Julie. I suffer from the process easily as much as you do. I have all I can do to keep myself together in the face of life. I can't save or rescue you.'

And in that instant I did understand. I had been nagging Tony because unconsciously I expected the man to take the lead, to give the answers, to come along on the white horse. And yet if he had done so, I would have hated him for condescending to me. And throughout all our changes, he steadfastly refused to play that part, and kept reminding me that I had to find my own source of salvation within myself.

I looked up at him and smiled, and in our exchange

of glances we said all that had to be said, for that crisis at any rate.

'Let's get some soda,' I said. 'And go watch television. It must be a fantastic program to pull you in there with such force.'

'It's an old-fashioned love story,' he said, 'about a man and a woman and their choice between romance and marriage.'

'Oh,' I replied, 'a comedy.'

But although we sat contentedly on the couch, holding hands and sipping our cokes, looking for all the world like any pair of newlyweds caught up in one another's vibration, a separate center had been born within me, an unsleeping eye. Without being able to pinpoint the precise second, somewhere during the year I had lost my innocence, and sometime during the night I had become aware of the fact.

I glanced over at the man sitting next to me, his face a show of shadow and light. Never had I been so close to a man, and never so distant at the same time.

I turned my head and watched the screen, wondering about the future, ready to open myself entirely to life, which had become something terribly real, fierce, vast, awesome, as necessary and as alien as the mysterious chasm between woman and man, the abyss which alone makes union possible.

More Erotic Fiction from Headline:

FOLLIES OF THE FLESH

ANONYMOUS

FOLLIES OF THE FLESH -

drunk on carnal pleasure and inspired by the foolish excitement of their lust, the crazed lovers in these four delightful, naughty, bawdy tales flaunt their passion shamelessly!

Randiana: the scandalous exploits of a witty young rogue whose wanton behaviour is matched only by his barefaced cheek...

The Autobiography of a Flea: the notorious misadventures of sweet young Bella, as chronicled by one who enjoys full knowledge of her most intimate desires...

The Lustful Turk: imprisoned in an Oriental harem, a passionate Victorian miss discovers a world of limitless sensual joy...

Parisian Frolics: in which the men and women of Parisian society cast off propriety and abandon themselves in an orgy of forbidden pleasure ...

Other classic erotic collections from Headline:
THE COMPLETE EVELINE
LASCIVIOUS LADIES
THE POWER OF LUST

FICTION/EROTICA   0 7472 3652 6

A selection of bestsellers from Headline

FICTION

GASLIGHT IN PAGE STREET	Harry Bowling	£4.99 ☐
LOVE SONG	Katherine Stone	£4.99 ☐
WULF	Steve Harris	£4.99 ☐
COLD FIRE	Dean R Koontz	£4.99 ☐
ROSE'S GIRLS	Merle Jones	£4.99 ☐
LIVES OF VALUE	Sharleen Cooper Cohen	£4.99 ☐
THE STEEL ALBATROSS	Scott Carpenter	£4.99 ☐
THE OLD FOX DECEIV'D	Martha Grimes	£4.50 ☐

NON-FICTION

THE SUNDAY TIMES SLIM PLAN	Prue Leith	£5.99 ☐
MICHAEL JACKSON The Magic and the Madness	J Randy Taraborrelli	£5.99 ☐

SCIENCE FICTION AND FANTASY

SORCERY IN SHAD	Brian Lumley	£4.50 ☐
THE EDGE OF VENGEANCE	Jenny Jones	£5.99 ☐
ENCHANTMENTS END Wells of Ythan 4	Marc Alexander	£4.99 ☐

All Headline books are available at your local bookshop or newsagent, or can be ordered direct from the publisher. Just tick the titles you want and fill in the form below. Prices and availability subject to change without notice.

Headline Book Publishing PLC, Cash Sales Department, PO Box 11, Falmouth, Cornwall, TR10 9EN, England.

Please enclose a cheque or postal order to the value of the cover price and allow the following for postage and packing:
UK & BFPO: £1.00 for the first book, 50p for the second book and 30p for each additional book ordered up to a maximum charge of £3.00.
OVERSEAS & EIRE: £2.00 for the first book, £1.00 for the second book and 50p for each additional book.

Name ....

Address ....

....

....